The Old Violin

Dorothy A. MacIntosh

 FriesenPress

Suite 300 - 990 Fort St
Victoria, BC, V8V 3K2
Canada

www.friesenpress.com

ISBN
978-1-5255-6724-7 (Hardcover)
978-1-5255-6725-4 (Paperback)
978-1-5255-6726-1 (eBook)

1. FICTION, CONTEMPORARY WOMEN

Distributed to the trade by The Ingram Book Company

Life is like playing a violin solo in public and learning the instrument as one goes.

Samuel Butler

Dedication

This book is dedicated to my husband
John Herbert MacIntosh
1925 - 2010

and my daughter
Linda Faye MacIntosh Sullivan
1956 - 2015

The Old Violin

THE SUN WAS RISING on the beautiful Middle River in Loch Broom, Pictou County, Nova Scotia. The many birds of the area were calling to each other, answering each other, and letting the world know that another day was dawning, and it was time to vacate your cozy bed and face the day, for time waits for no man, and time wasted is never regained.

Twenty-year-old Ann Blair took her usual early morning stroll, and on this stunningly, beautiful day ended up down by the river, as she did on frequent occasions, and took in the warm friendly surroundings. There was no other place in the universe that could give her more joy than this serene tract of land bordering the gentle flowing stream, making its way to Pictou Harbour and on into the Northumberland Strait.

Ann loved to call this cozy lacuna her own, for her many early morning visits here started her day with a feeling of anticipation as to what the day would bring. She was never disappointed with this start to her day.

Ann was presently on vacation from her studies at university, where she was pursuing her dream to be a teacher. She was visiting her grandmother, who lived in the old family farmhouse not very far from the river. She spent some time sitting on the warm sand, turning it over with her bare feet, and listening to the sounds of nature around her.

Time lost its meaning for her here, and she often spent an hour or more just relaxing in the warm sunshine. She spent these times dreaming of the things she would like to achieve in her lifetime. It was not her desire to be famous or honoured but just to help those less fortunate than herself and assist them in making their lives better.

Gradually, her thoughts returned to the present. She donned her comfortable sandals, arose, and walked slowly back to the house where she found her grandmother busily cooking breakfast for the two of them. Oatmeal porridge with brown sugar and cream was their usual morning fare, and they both sat at the kitchen table and engaged in some light, pleasant conversation as they enjoyed their meal.

Following this, Ann took her glass of orange juice, along with the daily newspaper, and left to sit beside a small table on the front deck and read the previous day's happenings.

Ann's grandmother's house was an old two-story farmhouse. On the bottom floor was a parlour, which was only used when the minister visited or some very special company (whom Grammie felt she should impress) called. The dining room was across the hall from the parlour, and it too was only used for special happenings. One reason for this was that it was so far from the kitchen where the food was prepared that one had to have their comfortable walking shoes on to make the trek. Besides that, in the winter the food would be cold by the time it reached the table.

The kitchen was the centre of the downstairs area, and just to one side of it was a bedroom. This was Grammie's bedroom, as she now found it difficult to climb the narrow stairway leading to the second floor. The back door to the outside was at the far end of the kitchen. The kitchen was the coziest part of the downstairs area, and Ann loved to spend time there with her grandmother.

The upper floor had four small bedrooms; three were just ordinary rooms but the fourth had always perplexed Ann. It had two windows, but neither one faced the outside of the house. One faced a window coming up the stairs, which gave some light to the room, and the other faced the area leading down the hall, which gave very little light to the room at all.

The visionary planning of the architect who drew up the design for the house must have had a special project for this room. However, not one of the occupants of the last hundred years could figure out what it was.

Ann finished her reading, and Grammie went out to work in her flower gardens. Ann sauntered up the stairs to make her bed and tidy up her bedroom. She finished her tasks and turned to go back downstairs. As she walked down the hall, she passed the room with the inside windows. She stopped and peered in one of them.

It was quite dark in there, and she could not see very well. There were several quite large trunks positioned close to the wall and behind them a number of boxes. Ann's imagination was running wild. She began to visualize some articles that might be hidden in those containers: clothing from days gone by perhaps, or pictures from past generations of her family and friends. How she would love to open those trunks and sort through the contents! She went to the door and turned the knob. The door would not open. It was locked.

This really surprised Ann. She went down the hall and sat on a chair at the far end of it.

"Why would someone lock that door?" she said out loud as though she were speaking to someone.

She continued to sit, and the questions went racing through her mind like wild fire. Why would her grandmother want to keep that door locked? Was there something in there she didn't want anyone to see? She was sure her grandmother had never done anything she would want to keep from her family or the law.

Maybe there was a family heirloom in there she wanted to preserve for a particular member of the family, and she was afraid someone would steal it. If that was the case, why didn't she give it to them now? She was getting up in years, and if there were any keepsakes she wished to go to certain people, it would be better to pass them out sooner rather than later. It was true Grammie was in good health still, but who knows?

Ann sat there for some time and then got up and went downstairs. The mystery of the contents of the room with no outside windows remained with Ann for the remainder of the day. She would love to know what was in that room and why the door was locked if it was not of value. She made a promise with herself that she would find the answer to the room's secrets before she left her grandmother's residence in less than a week.

Chapter 2

Secret Unveiled

TIME WAS QUICKLY PASSING for Ann, and her stay with her grandmother was starting to wind down. The mystery behind the locked door was still the main thing on her mind. She wanted to approach her grandmother about it but was unsure how to do it. She was certain Grammie would enlighten her, if she dared to ask, and otherwise, Ann had no idea how to get access to the strange room with no windows exposed to the outside of the house.

Ann pondered the enigma for one more day and then slowly an idea came to her. Each time she walked down the hall, she peered in through the window of the mysterious room, trying to find an exposed article that she might ask her grandmother about, hoping she would open the door and allow her to enter. Then all of a sudden, there it was. Almost buried behind the old trunks was a box that looked as though it might contain a musical instrument.

"Aha!" Ann said out loud. "This may be just what I need!"

Ann was not a musician by any stretch of the imagination, but she could play a few tunes on the violin, piano and could strum a bit on the guitar. She loved music, but the opportunity to take lessons and learn to play when she was younger had never presented itself. The little bit she did know she had picked up on her own on an old fiddle and guitar her father had when he was a boy. She had a good ear for music, which she'd probably inherited from her father who had learned to play by ear and was fairly good at it. Unfortunately, work and raising a family had prohibited him from continuing on with his interest in music, so he'd gladly let Ann try to learn to play using his beloved instruments.

Ann mulled the situation over in her mind. She wanted to be able to approach the subject with her grandmother and not sound too inquisitive or nosy. Before she could broach the subject, a perfect opportunity presented itself organically. She and her grandmother were sitting on the deck one evening, chatting away as they often did after supper and before bedtime.

Out of the blue, her grandmother asked her if she still played her father's violin. Ann told her grandmother that she didn't have much time for playing any more, but she would like to take a few lessons when time permitted.

"Grammie," she said, sitting back in her chair, "did anyone else in the family even play a musical instrument besides my dad?"

Grammie sat still for a moment, and then nodded slowly. "Yes, your great-grandfather Alex Blair did. He was a concert violinist and played for many years on stage across Canada and the United States.

"He was very well known for his musical ability. He passed away some time ago, in his late seventies, and his achievements were never talked much about. It seems a shame that a talented member of the family, such as he was, has been more or less forgotten about."

This was Ann's opportunity and she seized the moment. "What happened to his violin?"

Grammie moved about in her chair and shuffled her feet on the floor. "I believe his violin is here in the house."

"Oh, I would love to see it," said Ann. "Do you know where it is?"

"Yes, I think I do."

"Would it be possible for me to see it?"

"Yes, I believe so," her grandmother said. "However, I think it's in the room coming down the upstairs hall. The door is locked, and I can't find the key."

Ann's heart dropped. Perhaps she wouldn't get access into this puzzling room after all, and all because of a lost key. Well, she would help her grandmother find it. It had to be somewhere in the house. Surely no one would have thrown it out. It was quite likely her grandmother had placed the key where she would be sure to remember where it was and then completely forgotten where she had placed it. *Who knows?* she thought. *It might be close at hand.*

Ann felt that, if she put her thinking cap on, she could come up with places her grandmother might have placed the key for safe keeping.

She went to bed that evening with a note of determination in her mind. She would find that key. The good thing about the situation now was that she, at least, had a promise of entrance into that odd, old room.

The next morning, dawned bright and sunny. Ann was up at the crack of dawn and started her day on a mission. The number-one item on her mind was the key to the room she peered into each time she came down the hall. Where had her grandmother put that key? She had to think like an older person.

A younger person would be more likely to put the key on a key rack or ring with other keys, where as an older person might place the key in a flower pot on a nearby window sill or in an ornament on the living-room mantle. These places might make sense to one who had gotten up in years but quite foreign to one in a younger frame of mind.

The search was on. Ann felt like she could think old or young, but she only had two days left to find the key she needed to gain access to the room.

She asked her grandmother if she would give her permission to search some places in the house where she might have placed the key. Her grandmother was glad for the help, as she too was in a quandary, wondering where she may have put it. They spent most of the day checking areas of the house that were seldom visited but did not come up with the key—at least not the right old key.

Ann went to bed that night with fear in her heart that the sought-after key would not be uncovered before she had to leave, as she only had a short time left. She lay in bed, wide awake, trying to come up with some areas they had not visited. Ann still felt it was some place close at hand, likely a place where Grammie felt only she would know its whereabouts.

The last full day of Ann's vacation was here, and her attempt to locate the missing key was going to take top priority in the day's activities. She and her grandmother spent the complete day searching and racking their brains trying to come up with the answer, but to no avail. The key did not turn up and the time had come for Ann to pack her things and make ready for the trip back home.

She was so disappointed, and her grandmother felt sorry for her. Grammie was trying to think of something she could do to make Ann's last hours with her memorable. She sat on her old rocker on the front deck and tried to think of something she could give Ann that would take her mind off the lost key.

All of a sudden, it hit her. She knew exactly what would soften the disappointment of not finding the key Ann wanted. Ann finished her packing and returned downstairs to sit with Grammie on the deck. Grammie could see how letdown Ann was feeling and decided to try to cheer her up.

"Ann," she said, "I have something I want to give you. It's a cameo broach that belonged to my mother, your great-grandmother. I have kept it all these years, and it was always my intention to one day give it to you. I think the time has come. I will have to ask you to get it for me, as I would have to climb up on a chair to get it. Take one of the kitchen chairs, stand on it, and go to the top shelf in the pantry. There is an old sugar bowl there. Would you bring it to me?"

Ann did as her grandmother requested. She stood on a chair and searched the top shelf. Sure enough, there it was, almost completely hidden from view. The old chipped sugar bowl looked like it had not been used for years. Ann returned and handed it to her grandmother, then placed the chair back in the kitchen and came back and sat down.

Grammie sat for a minute with the sugar bowl in her hand before she took the top off and removed a small box. It was old and had a cover topped with a small purple bow. The corners of the box were worn bare, giving it the appearance of having been handled many times. She opened the box and removed the broach.

Ann let out a gasp. It was beautiful. She couldn't believe how lucky she was to be given this family heirloom. She would treasure it forever. She rushed over to her grandmother and threw her arms around her. Both of them shed some tears. It brought back happy times for Grammie, and she was so pleased to pass it on to a beloved granddaughter.

Ann took the broach from Grammie and placed it back in the box, holding it in her hand as though it were the most precious gift she would ever receive. Then Ann noticed the sugar bowl was not empty. There was a wad of tissue paper in the bottom.

She reached in and pulled the paper out, then heard a "clink" as something hit the floor. Ann and Grammie both looked down at the same instant. There, lying on the floor, was a key.

Could this be the key they were searching for? They both sat still, not believing what they were seeing. Ann picked the key up and handed it to her grandmother. She could see her thinking. Was she remembering that she had placed the key there for safe keeping and had completely forgotten about it until she saw it on the floor?

Ann could tell by the look on her grandmother's face that the memory was returning. Grammie said nothing. She raised herself from her chair, slowly entered the house, and made her way up the narrow staircase. She walked to the door of the darkened room and inserted the key into the lock. There was a soft "click." Then she turned the knob and the door opened.

Finally, Ann had access to the room that had intrigued her for the past ten days. With the permission of her grandmother, she could sift through some of the room's contents.

Grammie returned to her seat on the deck, leaving Ann to go through whatever boxes she wanted or needed to. She wanted to think about when she had put the key there and why. Perfect quietness would now be her friend, and with this, she was sure the memory would return.

Ann turned on the old table lamp in the corner and stood for a moment until her eyes became accustomed to the dim light. She then walked over to one of the trunks and raised the top. Sure enough, it contained what she had imagined when she viewed the old container through the window: clothes from a different era. To someone in the theatre business, this trunk and its contents would have been a treasure trove, but to Ann, they were just old clothes.

She closed the trunk top and opened another one. With the exception of a few old, interesting family pictures on the top, which she promised herself to view later, it too was full of old clothes from the past. She opened several more old trunks and boxes, but there was nothing that piqued her interest.

Then she remembered the old violin box half hidden behind the trunks. She moved one of the trunks and pulled the box out from its resting place. Part of the box was laden with dust and obviously had not been opened for some time. She laid the case on top of one of the trunks and toyed with one of the clasps on the side. It was not going to open easily, and it took her many tries before it slowly let go of its grasp with a raspy sound.

The second clasp opened much easier, and Ann slowly opened the old case. Inside was an old violin, which had seen better days. To someone in days gone by, it was probably a cherished instrument, but it was quite evident that those days were in the past, and it was now, almost, just a piece of old junk in an old room in an old house.

Chapter 3

Missing Parts

ANN STOOD AND LOOKED at what she had just uncovered for a minute or two. She knew only a few things about a violin but she knew enough to know that many parts of this particular one were either unattached or missing. She picked it up and turned it over in her hands.

The bridge was not there, and the tailpiece was unattached. The G and A strings were loose and the E string was missing. One of the tuning pegs was missing too, and another one was in the old case. The fingerboard looked as though it might be better than the other parts. The chin rest and fine tuners were long gone. The sound post was there though, and the belly of the old instrument was in perfect shape. It didn't have a scratch on it.

Ann could not understand why an instrument of great value to someone, which she suspected this had been at one time, would be left in such a state. She took it closer to the light, held it up and peered through the "F" holes. There was some printing on the inside. She moved the violin around several times so she could see the printing clearly. It read - "Nicalaus Amatus fecit - Cremona 16."

This had very little meaning to Ann, but she was determined to find out the significance of it. She placed the old instrument back in its case, and tucked it under her arm. Then she toted it with her as she turned off the light and carried it out into the hall and down the stairs.

She found Grammie back on the deck. Many questions popped into her mind, and she could not help but wonder if Grammie was up to answering them. She sat down next to her grandmother with the old violin case on her knee.

Grammie looked at her for a few seconds. "Oh my goodness," she said, "I see you've found it."

"Yes," answered Ann. "This old violin has piqued my interest. I'd like to know the story behind it."

Grammie shifted in her chair, and Ann could tell the story was coming back to her. She waited for a few minutes and slowly Grammie began to speak.

"I told you that your great-grandfather Alex Blair was a great concert violinist. Well, this was his violin. He was a heavy smoker and died from lung cancer in his late seventies, leaving a wife and two grown children, Herbert and George. One of those children was your grandfather, George Blair.

"The last year or so before Alex passed away, he came to live here with my husband, George and I, and his belongings came with him.

Some of the clothes you saw in the old trunks were his, and of course, so was the violin.

"When he passed away, his belongings were left here and placed in the room where you found them. During their summer vacations, some of the grandchildren, your cousins, would come and were allowed access to that room. They often played in there and eventually everything became a mess.

"The last time they were allowed in, I cleaned everything up as soon as they left and noticed the awful condition the violin was in. I placed it in the case, with all the missing pieces I could find, and shoved it in behind the trunks. It has remained there until now. Then I locked the door.

"Please take it. Perhaps you could have it repaired to its original shape and even learn to play it. Your father was quite musical. He had a great ear, and even though he didn't have any formal training, he was very good on the violin."

Ann was overjoyed. It might not have been the most valuable violin in the world, but it was to her. She vowed she would restore it to its original shape and learn to play it. She felt she would never be a great violinist like her great-grandfather, but she would at least learn to play a tune or two on it.

The following morning, Grammie told Ann she remembered why the key to that room was in the sugar bowl. She said that, as soon as she'd finished cleaning the room, she had wanted to put the key where only she knew where it was, so that on future visits, Ann's cousins could no longer get into that room. They visited again on many occasions but found the door locked, and of course, it was to *stay* locked, since even Grammie forgot where she put the key.

That day, Ann returned to her home with the broken violin in her possession. She was delighted that her grandmother had allowed her to keep it.

Home Again

IN EARLY SEPTEMBER, ANN returned to university to complete her final year. She loved her studies there and attacked them with enthusiasm. During this final year, she would spend much of her time doing practice teaching in the many schools in the surrounding area, and her final three weeks would be spent at a school of her choice.

Ann loved her studies, but more than anything, she loved the "practice teaching." She was in her glory when standing in front of a class and talking with students, instructing them and answering their questions. She found their enthusiasm delightful and very rewarding. There was nothing that gave Ann more pleasure than enlightening young minds and helping to carve their paths into the future. Being a teacher also meant always learning along with the students, and she liked that challenge.

Ann had very little free time until Thanksgiving weekend. She came home for the three days she had free from classes. It was so nice to be with her parents again and have her mother dote on her as she always did. To Ann, coming home meant sleeping in for an hour or two in the morning and then enjoying a late breakfast. There was nothing Ann enjoyed more, and she took advantage of it when she got the chance.

After breakfast, Ann went back to her bedroom to make her bed, and to have a shower and wash her hair. Later, having completed these personal tasks, she went to put some things away in her closet and the first thing to catch her eye was the old violin case.

She picked it up and carried it to her bed. She stood and gazed at it for a minute and then opened the case. A feeling of sadness came over her as she remembered what her grandmother had told her about the former owner of the old instrument. This was an instrument that had played glorious music at the hands of a talented musician. It now lay in ruins at the hands of children who didn't know its value.

At that very instant, Ann made up her mind to restore it to its original shape. An instrument with the history and sound that this one had should not be allowed to stay in this state of disrepair. She closed the case and made up her mind that she would take it with her back to university and locate someone who was knowledgeable about violins and could restore it to the way it had been when it was played by her great-grandfather.

The three days Ann had at home were pleasant and restful and passed all too quickly. Tuesday of that week found her back at university and mired down with numerous assignments, tests, and practice teaching. She seldom had moments to herself, and for the time being, the old violin was put on the "back burner" again.

The winter passed quickly for Ann. It was not an easy winter for her as she boarded with a family whose house gave her a fair distance to walk every day to and from the university. Since the students at this institution had an hour and a half off at noon each day, she walked home for lunch and made the trip back again for one thirty in the afternoon.

Classes usually ended for the day at four o'clock, unless one had a lab class, which could go much later. It was a long day. Easter vacation was coming up when Ann remembered she had still not taken the violin to be restored. She was not too familiar with the music stores in the area, so she pondered what to do. Suddenly an idea came to her. She would ask Mr. Ainsley, the music teacher at the university. She felt he would be able to advise her on what was the best road to take in order to mend the old violin. Ann made an appointment to see him and looked forward to his recommendations.

The appointment date arrived, and Ann told Mr. Ainsley her story. He was very interested in what she had to say. He asked her great-grandfather's name, and Ann told him it was Alex Blair. Mr. Ainsley had taken a course on local musicians and the name seemed familiar to him. He told her he would do some research on the gentleman. However, she needed some advice right now, and he was lost in thought for a few minutes.

Finally, he said, "I wouldn't recommend you taking it to one of the music stores here, not because they're not good at what they do but because they run a business and will repair it and give it back to you as just part of another day's work. I would advise you to take it to a gentleman I know. He's a violin maker in his own right. He makes very good instruments and has a great amount of knowledge in this area. I'm sure he'd be extremely interested in your violin and will do his best to put it back to its original condition."

Ann agreed to this. She felt he knew best. Besides, he seemed very interested in her story, and she felt he was advising her wisely.

Mr. Ainsley added, "The man's name is Jack MacGuire, and he lives in the area, not too far from here. I'll call him and set up an appointment for you. What would be a good day for your schedule?"

Ann thought for a few seconds and said a Saturday would be the best for her. He agreed to try to get her an appointment on the nearest Saturday possible. Ann thanked him for his help and went on with her day's activities, pleased with his assistance.

Mr. Ainsley was successful in obtaining an appointment for Ann on the following Saturday, and with the old violin in hand, Ann arrived at the scheduled time. After introductions were made and Ann had thanked him for meeting with her, she opened the case and left it for him to peruse. He looked at it for a moment. It was not a pleasing sight for someone who spent a good amount of his time making and restoring violins. He picked the violin up and sat down.

Ann watched him as he surveyed the situation. He looked everything over for several minutes before he spoke a word.

"It certainly needs some repair," he said as he took note of the many parts that had to be put back into place.

"It seems like this might be a fairly good instrument, but time will tell. Leave it with me, and I'll try to restore it so that it can be played again. It's a very old violin as far as I can tell. It may be a few days before I can work on it though, as I have some others in the works now. I'll call you in a week or so."

Ann was satisfied with that. She thanked him and left for her boarding house. Now that the violin was taken care of, she could concentrate on her studies.

Easter vacation was upon her almost before she had time to think about it. She had some big assignments to complete, so she packed them to take home with her to work on over the holidays. It felt good to be home again for a few days, away from the busy routine she faced every day at university.

She thoroughly enjoyed her days away from her studies. She loved to go for long walks in the snow. She dressed warmly, as the days were still quite cold, put the family dog on his leash, and took him along for company. He enjoyed the romp in the snow as much as she did. Upon their return, Ann was exhilarated from her walk, and the dog soon settled on a mat in the kitchen for a nap.

Ah, the simple things in life are good, she thought, as she went to her room to work on her assignments

Vacation passed too quickly, and soon Ann was back at university for her final three months. It was near the middle of May before Jack

MacGuire called Ann to tell her that her violin was ready. She made an appointment for the following weekend, and Saturday of that week found her at Mr. MacGuire's home.

Ann was delighted when she saw the old violin. It now looked like a violin should. All the pieces were back in place, and the missing ones had been replaced. She found it hard to believe the old gentleman had made such a change in the almost ruined relic she had delivered to him a few short weeks ago. What a nice surprise! She picked up the bow and looked it over. It had been restored to its original state. It almost looked like a new bow. Ann was thrilled with the results.

Mr. MacGuire could see she was very pleased with his efforts and that gave him a very satisfied feeling. He told her he had tuned it but that it must be played to stay in tune, especially since it now had all new strings. He handed her the violin and asked her to try it. She told him she was not very good but could play a tune or two.

She took the instrument from him and did her best to play a tune she knew fairly well. It was a loud violin and had a tone all its own. It had once been a cherished instrument of a former concert violinist and now she knew why. She vowed right there and then that she would learn to play it properly.

Ann placed the violin in its old case, covered it with a cloth that came with it, fastened the bow in the lid of the case, and closed it. Then she paid Mr. MacGuire, thanked him for his efforts, and carried the old violin to her car.

Ann graduated in June of that year. She had a job teaching grade-nine mathematics at Wellspring Academy in Lawson Brook, Nova Scotia, in the coming school year. She moved her belongings home for the summer, and among them was her precious old violin. All was right with her world.

First Job

ANN SPENT MOST OF the summer at home with her parents. Some mornings she slept in as she knew that, when she started her new job in September, it would not be a luxury she would be able to do very often. Some mornings though, she was up early and went for a long walk with Jake, the family dog. This was one of her favourite morning activities, and the dog liked it as well.

Near the middle of July, Ann visited her grandmother and spent two weeks with her. Her morning walks to the Middle River near Grammie's house were still one of her preferred morning activities, and she tried to do it every day, weather permitting. She usually sat on an available rock and wiggled her toes in the warm sand. It gave her the feeling of total peace and relaxation. It was one of the things she really enjoyed when she visited her grandmother, as it was not always easy to do in her everyday life. After some time, she would wander back to the house and enjoy breakfast with Grammie.

Following breakfast on her first morning with Grammie, she had gone up to her bedroom and come back with the old violin. She had brought it with her to show her grandmother the change she had made in it.

Grammie sat in anticipation as Ann opened the aged case and unveiled the old instrument. Her grandmother was in awe. She could not believe the change in it since it had left her house with Ann the previous summer. She took it from Ann and turned it over in her hands.

"How did you make such a change in it?" she asked.

Ann told her that she had taken it to a violin maker and repair man in an area close to where she boarded and that he had repaired it for her. Grammie was completely surprised and overwhelmed with joy to see the old violin back in its original form. She handed it back to Ann, who returned it to the case.

Grammie looked at the old case, with its corners worn and clasps that were difficult to open. "All it needs now is a new case. Could I give you the money to buy a nice new case for it?"

"Oh, no!" answered Ann. "I'll buy a new case for it. I want to take lessons and learn to read music. Let that be my responsibility. You gave me the violin, and I really appreciate that. However, there is something you can do for me. Perhaps you could sit down and write up the history of the violin. Tell me the story of Alex Blair and his life as a concert violinist. I would love to know the story, and so would my music teacher at the university. It would be great to take the true story to him."

Grammie said that she certainly could do that. It would take her some time to gather all the information she needed, but she had kept clippings of his playing over the years, and the family could also contribute.

"Just leave that with me. I will do my best," she said.

Ann stayed with her grandmother for almost two weeks and then went back home to prepare for her job that was beginning the first of September.

The month of August slipped by very quickly, and the first of September found Ann in her new home. She'd rented a small house near the school and arrived a week early to get settled in. She spent her first mornings at the school getting used to finding her way around the buildings and putting things in order for teaching. The complex consisted of a large main building, an annex, and two sets of portable classrooms. It was a little puzzling until one got used to the setup.

Ann's classroom was in the main building, so finding her way around was not too much of a problem. She was one of the lucky ones, as all the grade nines were in the main building. Those teachers who were teaching grades seven, eight, some grade tens, and those students learning secretarial skills were not so lucky. They had further to travel, especially if they had to visit the main office, which was in the main building.

Ann visited the office on her first visit to the school and got all the information she needed for the time being. She worked in her room, and many of the teachers dropped by to introduce themselves and offer their assistance if she needed help. The turn over of staff at the school each year was not great, so most of the teaching staff were very glad to assist new teachers should the need arise.

It took a week to get her classroom in order and things prepared for the first few days of classes. She worked on that in the mornings and used the afternoons to get her household items in proper place. She made a trip to the nearest store for groceries and planned a dinner menu for the following week. Breakfast was usually cereal or toast, and lunch was a sandwich, but she liked to make a proper meal for dinner.

School started on a Thursday, and she was up bright and early, ready to start her teaching career. She was new at the job, and like all teachers starting their first term, she was a little anxious about what the day might bring. Ann got through the day with very few worrisome incidents, and at the end of it, she was told by an older and more experienced teacher that she had just completed her worst day of the whole school year. That bit of information made her feel much better. If all her teaching days were no worse than her first day, then she might be able to handle her chosen career.

Teaching grade-nine mathematics was no walk in the park. It was a tough job. Ann had five grade-nine classes, and each class had six periods a cycle. The school was on a five-day cycle, so that meant she taught thirty classes each cycle, with five periods for marking, grading, and preparation.

She was soon to find out that marking, grading, and preparation took much more time than that, so a good amount had to be done after hours or at home. Since this was her first year of teaching, those activities took much more time than she had anticipated, and she spent many hours in preparation on the weekend and sometimes late at night during the week.

Ann did not shrink from her duties, and working hard was not foreign to her. Her main concerns were her students and her desire to be the best teacher she could be for them. If a student needed extra help, Ann made herself available as often as was possible. She stayed after school as much as she could, but her weekends were her own. She felt she needed some down time in order to do her best job. Besides, she had a house to look after and shopping to do, and these tasks were a necessity as well as a break from her teaching. She needed that.

On one of her weekends, Ann was straightening up her closet when she picked up the old violin. She remembered that she had promised Grammie that she was going to buy a new case for it. Right there and then, she decided this was the day to do it. She made herself presentable, picked up the old violin and her car keys, and headed for New Glasgow.

She found the only music store in New Glasgow and entered with violin in hand. She explained to the clerk that she wanted a good case for her violin. The clerk was very helpful and showed her several they had on hand. She chose one of the more expensive ones, as she felt this old violin deserved the best. She paid for it, thanked the clerk, picked up the old case as well as her new one, and drove home.

As she entered the house, the phone was ringing. She set the two cases on the kitchen table and ran to answer it. Her mother was calling, and after some time on the phone, she removed her jacket and returned to the kitchen. It was getting late in the day, so she took the two cases and carried them to the hall closet.

Ann was not accustomed to living alone and having to do everything herself. Teaching took most of her time but cleaning, laundry, and cooking meals were a necessity as well. She had to get organized to handle these activities. She was working on it, but it was taking time to adjust to this part of her life, and it was not easy for her.

It was well into the month of December before she had reasonably conquered a routine to take care of the necessities of her life away from teaching. However, it would take her a few more months before everything really fell into place and things began to run more smoothly.

Christmas came and went. Ann went home to be with her parents for a few days, but to her surprise, she found that she was glad to get back to her own home and return to her regular routine. She was hanging a new coat her parents had given her for Christmas in the hall closet when she noticed the two violin cases.

She stared at them for a moment or two. She had completely forgotten about putting them there. She picked them up and carried them to the kitchen table. She viewed the new case she had bought and was again pleased with her purchase. She thought it really suited the instrument it contained, and that anyone would be proud to carry their violin in it. She set it to one side.

The old case looked very shabby and kind of sad compared to the newly purchased one. It made Ann feel rather triste when she thought of the past glorious days that case would have been a part of. The case had been to many important concerts with the old violin within, and now it lay in almost complete shambles. To do away with it seemed an unhappy ending to this historic and once-handsome container. She just could not part with it.

She opened the case to view the inside. It was lined with a red velvet material that must have looked really posh in the beginning. A box lined in this way made a perfect space to protect a prize instrument such as the one carried in this old case. She stood and looked at the inside of it for a few minutes, when all at once, her eyes were drawn to a spot at the top of the case. The velvet was pulled away from the top edge, and there seemed to be a small gap there.

She stuck one of her fingers into the space and moved it around as best she could. She felt something. It seemed like it was a piece of paper. She had to get at least two fingers into the gap before she could retrieve whatever was there. With two fingers, she managed to grab what seemed to be a sheet of paper, but she had to enlarge the gap before she managed to pull it out.

Ann was very excited with her discovery, even though at the beginning she didn't know what she had found. She unfolded the sheet of paper, and to her surprise, it was a hand-written piece of music. The title at the top of the page read "The Old Violin."

Ann could read enough music to realize that it was a very simple tune and probably one she (and the music world) had never heard. The bottom of the sheet had the words "Composed by Alex Blair."

Ann stood in complete surprise. This was a piece of music written by her great-grandfather! She made a decision right at that instant that she would learn to read music and play the tune composed by her great-grandfather. She took the old violin case, carried it back to the hall closet, and placed it at the back of the top shelf. She vowed that, as long as she was around, that case would stay in the family.

Chapter 6

Music Classes Begin

ANN SPENT SOME TIME searching before she found a music teacher who was not booked solid with students. Finally, she found a retired teacher who took a few adult students each year, and she agreed to take Ann on as a pupil.

On a clear cold evening in the middle of January, Ann carried her old violin with the shiny new case to her first lesson. Her teacher was a Mrs. Elsa Smith, a widow in her late sixties, who lived alone in a pleasant old house in Stellarton. The slim woman took a few students each year just to give her something to do. Having taught untalented and uninterested students in school for years, it was a great pleasure to share her gifts, in piano and violin, with people who genuinely wanted to learn.

On the first evening of her class, Ann told Mrs. Smith her story. She found that her teacher was very interested, as Elsa had come across the name "Alex Blair" through her teaching. Elsa asked many questions, some of which Ann could not answer. However, she told Elsa that her grandmother was going to write the story up for her, and that she would give it to Elsa when it was finished.

Ann uncovered her violin, and Elsa was very impressed. Ann handed it to her, and she carefully surveyed the old instrument, asking many questions as she did so. Ann explained to her how she happened to be the one to acquire it and that, now that she had it, she wanted to learn to play.

Elsa immediately took her as a student. She gave Ann her first lesson that very evening. Right away, Elsa could see that Ann was going to be a good student. She had a natural ability and a good ear. Learning to play the violin was not going to be very difficult for her. Elsa went over the parts of the violin and gave her some easy tunes to start with. Ann had a good feeling about her time with Elsa and was looking forward to her next visit.

Ann found herself very active for the remainder of the school term. Teaching, housekeeping, and now her violin lessons, which she dearly loved, kept her very busy. For now, her teaching and her students were her main concern, but she was very happy during the times when she found a few minutes in her busy schedule to take out her violin and practice the pieces her teacher gave her with each lesson. She was progressing very well, in fact, better than most of the students Elsa had ever taught. She had a natural ability, and Elsa figured it had probably been inherited from her great-grandfather.

There were some very engaging days as the school term ended. Finally, the hectic days were over, and Ann could find some time to relax. Her first year of teaching was a learning experience but successful, and she was told by older instructors that she had just completed her worst year. Every year from now on would get easier, as she settled into a routine. Ann was pleased to hear that.

Finally, she could concentrate on her violin. Lessons were over for the summer; however, her teacher had given her some pieces to work on, and Ann could not wait to get started on them. She set her music stand up in the room she used as a study, and every time she had a few minutes, she could be found practicing.

She had most of the pieces she had to learn on tape, and as soon as she learned to play them by note, she would play along with the tape. Using this method, and with her keen ear, she was able to learn them and play them to perfection. Ann was a perfectionist in this area, and if it was not perfect, she was not happy. She practiced until it was flawless.

In late July, Ann made a trip to Loch Broom to visit her grandmother. She often called her to make sure that she was all right, or if she needed anything, but Grammie would have nothing to do with cell phones or computers. She was from the old school. The house phone was good enough for her.

Grammie was delighted with Ann's visit and really surprised to see her carrying the old violin in its shiny new case. Grammie immediately asked what she had done with the old case, and Ann told her not to worry; she had tucked it away for safe keeping. It carried a great deal of history, and she was not about to throw it away.

Ann wondered why her grandmother seemed to look relieved, especially as she had been the first to suggest that it needed a new case, but she immediately put the thought out of her mind.

On the first morning after arriving at her grandmother's home, Ann did what she always did. She got up early and made her way to the Middle River. She sat in the sand, kicked off her sandals, and wiggled her feet in the warm sand. It was so peaceful here, and she just sat in the warm sunshine, listened to the birds, and watched the water ripple by as it made its way to Pictou Harbour.

She heard a rustle in the bushes behind her and turned to see a mother deer and her baby walk slowly to the water for a drink. The deer did not see her, and Ann watched the little one tease its mother while it waded around in the water. After a few minutes, the two slowly wandered back into the bushes, and she heard them move away.

She spent about an hour just sitting in the sand and drinking in the solitude and peace. Slowly, she realized Grammie would be wondering if she was alright, so she slipped her sandals on and walked back to the house.

As she entered, she saw that Grammie had breakfast ready. Ann and her grandmother chatted away as they ate breakfast, following which Ann cleaned up and washed the dishes. She tidied up the kitchen and then she and Grammie headed off in separate directions to do some chores.

Once she had finished her tasks, Ann picked up her violin and carried it downstairs and out onto the deck, where she found Grammie sitting in her rocking chair.

"It makes me feel so good to see you take an interest in the violin," Grammie said. "Can you play something for me? I haven't heard that violin played for many years."

Ann removed the violin from the case, made sure it was in tune, and played a few pieces she was sure Grammie would know. Her grandmother was really surprised that Ann could play so well. After all, she only had the instrument for a short time. After Ann had played several more pieces, she played the piece of music she had found tucked away in the old violin case.

When Ann finished the piece, Grammie sat there with a look of complete shock on her face.

"Where did you get that piece of music?" she asked. "That tune was written by your great-grandfather, but it was never published. I remember when he wrote it. He often played it for us when he visited. I loved to hear him play it. The melody is so beautiful. I'd never heard anything like it before. It's the type of tune you never forget. Would you play it again for me?"

Ann really liked the piece of music as well, and she loved to play it. She was pleased that her grandmother liked it, and she played it again for her. Grammie was so pleased to hear someone in the family bring that piece of music back.

"Tell me, Ann," she said, "where did you find the music for that tune?"

Ann explained that she had found it in the lining of the old violin case.

"Was there anything else there?" she asked.

"Not that I know of," answered Ann. "Why do you ask?"

"I don't know, but I have a feeling there may have been something else in that old case. I have been trying to find all the information I can on your great-grandfather, and there seems to be some pieces of information missing. I just feel there is some of the story hidden somewhere, and I am trying to think where that might be.

"When you go home, take a closer look in the old case. There may be something else you could have overlooked."

Ann tucked that request away in her mind and vowed that she would do some more investigating just as soon as she got home. She had to admit that she hadn't thought to do any further inspecting after she had found the music. She'd been very surprised to find anything at all, so any further scrutiny had not even crossed her mind.

"How much information did you find?" she asked her grandmother.

"Quite a lot," answered Grammie, "but nothing out of the ordinary. There was a lot of the everyday things one would expect, and a great deal on his travels with his music, but there is a small time in his life where there is some information missing. I have never heard other members of the family mention anything out of the ordinary, but they did not always keep in touch with him. He was a bit secretive at times.

Have a look for me. Perhaps there's nothing there, but maybe there is. It's worth a look."

This bit of information was quite interesting to Ann, and she was looking forward to returning home and going through the old violin case again. Ann remained with her grandmother for another week and then returned home. She opened the windows and doors when she got there, to air the house as the weather had been unusually hot and the house was very stuffy.

She unpacked her suitcases, put her dirty clothes in the washer, and started it. After changing into more comfortable clothes and checking the mail, she finished tidying up, and in doing so, she went to put her violin where she usually kept it. Then she remembered that she had promised her grandmother to check the old violin case for any further information.

Ann found it a bit exciting and a little mysterious to be bringing out the old violin case again. She took it down from the shelf where she remembered putting it and placed it on the table in the kitchen. She slowly opened the clasps on the side and lifted the lid. She located the opening from which she had retrieved the paper with the music on it and tried to slide her hand down into the bottom of the case. She wiggled her hand back and forth but could only get about halfway down. She pulled her hand out and made the opening larger. Then she shoved her hand back into the larger opening, and it was much easier to explore the inside of the case.

She was about two thirds of the way down when she felt something.

Again, it seemed to be sheets of paper. It took her a minute or two to get hold of them, pinching them between two fingers as the lining was too tight to allow her to bend her hand enough to get her thumb to work. After several attempts, she managed to get a good enough hold on them, and they started to move. It took a couple more tries, but she finally managed to bring them to daylight.

Ann found she had several sheets of paper neatly pressed together. It was quite evident they had been there for some time. The paper had turned quite yellow and some of the print was getting faint but was entirely readable. Ann was so excited that she could barely hold the papers. Her hands shook as she sat down to see what she had actually uncovered.

She unfolded the papers one at a time. The first one was a deed to a cottage and fifty acres of land in Guysborough County in Nova Scotia. It was near the village of Boylston, in a seemingly remote area near the Milford Haven River, possibly overlooking it. The cottage belonged to her great-grandfather Alex Blair. She assumed he'd bought it after his wife, Ann's great-grandmother, had passed away.

Ann had never been to Guysborough County, so she was unaware of where the cottage was located. However, she was determined to find out. She put the deed aside and unfolded the second sheet of paper. It contained the number of a bank account in the Bank of Nova Scotia in Antigonish. The account was in her great-grandfather's name. The third sheet was a letter, which gave the cottage and the bank account to the person, in the Blair family, who found and kept the old violin in good shape and learned to play it. The paper was dated and signed by her great-grandfather Alex Blair.

Ann could not believe what she had just found. This was truly history and would certainly add to her grandmother's story on the life of Alex Blair, the great violinist. She read the papers for the second time, then she ran to the phone and called Grammie.

Grammie must have been sitting close to the phone as she answered right away.

"Hello?"

"Hi, Grammie, this is Ann. Remember you told me to have another look in the old violin case to see if there was anything else there?"

"Yes, I do."

"Well, I did as you asked. I went into the lining of the old violin case and found some papers. They look very important to me. I am going to come right over to show them to you. Is that okay with you?"

"Yes, yes!" exclaimed Grammie. "Oh, please come right over. I am so excited. I won't be able to sleep tonight if I don't find out what you found. I just made a pan of biscuits, and I will put the teapot on. See you soon."

Ann placed the papers in her purse. Then she grabbed her house keys, car keys, jacket, and purse and was out the door in a flash. She knew her grandmother, and waiting was not one of her best qualities.

It only took about twenty minutes to drive to Grammie's house, and Grammie was at the door when she arrived. Upon entering her grandmother's home, she gave Grammie a kiss, then removed her jacket, pulled the papers from her purse, and handed them to Grammie.

Grammie sat down by the kitchen table. Ann had the papers in the order she'd found them, so Grammie saw the deed first. She read it through and laid it down on the table, removing her glasses.

"Well," she said, "this may answer some of the questions that I've been pondering as I was trying to write the story of his life. There were a number of years after his wife died when there was no mention of his having played anywhere, and I wondered where he had gone. Now I know. He obviously wanted to be alone with his music, so he bought the cottage in a remote area where few people would know him or had even heard of him. I drove through Boylston a number of years ago. However, all I can say is that I have an idea where it is on the map."

Grammie picked up the paper with the bank account number on it and the location of the account.

"This too answers a question, as we knew your great-grandfather had some money. We had no idea how much, but we knew there had to be some in a bank somewhere. I wonder who is to receive his money."

Then Grammie picked up the third sheet of paper and read it.

"Well, my dear," she said, looking at Ann, "this answers my last question. The whole thing belongs to you. You were the one who brought the old violin back to life, and you were the one in the family who learned to play it. If it were not for you, that old violin would still be lodged behind a trunk in that room upstairs. There is no argument here.

"You are a member of the family, and you found them, so they are left to you. He must have been seeing into the future and knew that someday one of his heirs would play that violin and the piece of music he composed. He was a clever man. What better way to give it to the right person than the way he did it? Congratulations, my dear. It's yours!"

Ann sat there in complete silence. It took a few minutes for this to sink in. She was the owner of the violin, the cottage, and the bank account. They were all hers. *Wow! What a difference a day makes!* Ann was very excited with her find. She was now a land owner. She liked the sound of that.

Grammie sat thinking for a few minutes and Ann just let her be. Then Grammie began to talk.

"Ann, I want you to take those papers to a lawyer and have them made legal. There is no doubt the cottage, land, bank account, and violin are yours, but you know that in this family, as in many families, there is always someone who will try to contest your ownership of these findings. Make it all yours, for that is who it belongs to. If you can't afford a lawyer, I will give you the money."

It was true that Ann didn't have much money to pay for extras at the present time. She had loans from her university days, and her salary for the first few years of teaching was not huge, but she was sure she could handle it. She certainly did not want to take her grandmother's money.

"Grammie," she said, "thank you for the good advice, but I don't want to take your money. I think I can look after it. I will take it to a lawyer right away. I agree that it's best to have it in my name before anyone knows about it. Most members of the family would not be interested, but I know there's one who would do whatever she could to cause trouble, and she's the one least deserving of anything."

Ann promised her grandmother that she would look after the matter right away. She stayed for another hour or so, gave her Grammie a hug, and headed for her home.

Chapter 7

Life Goes On

THERE WAS ONE WEEK left before school started for the term. Ann had things almost ready. She had to make a few visits to the school to get her classroom set up and ready for students. She had to get her timetable and class lists for the coming year. She liked to be prepared and ready. It was essential to her to be a step ahead of her students before they entered her classroom.

She took Monday and Tuesday of the week following her visit to Grammie's to visit the school. She had already made an appointment with Ira Harris, a lawyer in the area, to attend to the papers she had found. Wednesday morning of the same week found her in his office. After introductions, she told him her story and presented him with the papers.

Mr. Harris asked many questions as to where she had found them, how she happened to have the violin, and what had provoked her to look inside the lining of the case in the first place. Ann took her time and told him the whole story, from the reason why the case was in her grandmother's house right up to finding the papers.

Mr. Harris listened to her story and found it very interesting. He had heard of Alex Blair, the local violinist, but hadn't realized his relatives were so close by. Hearing the story from someone closely related to him and getting the story firsthand was a treat.

"Thank you for telling me the story in such detail," he said. "I'll take a look at what you've found. It may take a little time, as I will have to check the deeds to the property and the details on the bank account, but then I'll get back to you."

"Are these papers I found legally binding?" Ann asked.

"It was apparently his wish that the property, cabin, bank account, and violin were to go to the person who found them and learned to play the violin. All of it was to go to that same person, and you are that person. He signed the papers and dated them, so I can't see them not being legally binding. I will check it out thoroughly though, and get back to you as soon as I can."

Ann thanked him and left his office. She went home quite satisfied that the matter was in good hands.

School opened the first of September, and the weather was beautiful, making it quite certain that most students would be reluctant to return to classes. Of course, this made it more difficult for teachers to get their undivided attention. The first day, as all teachers know, is the worst day, and after that things settle into a routine.

Ann was well prepared and her classes ran smoothly. Most of her students were ready to learn, and because of her preparations for the courses she was allotted for the year, students under her supervision were given the best of instruction. This was her second year of teaching, and the experienced teachers had been right when they'd told her the first year would be the worst. Now that she had some experience and was familiar with the way the school operated, she felt more comfortable in her job. She was more confident in her teaching and had now become more at ease as she started each day.

September and October slid by, and Ann still hadn't heard from her lawyer. She began to wonder if there were some roadblocks in his endeavour to settle her ownership of the cabin and the land that was part of it. Perhaps the bank was unwilling to release the bank account. She felt the violin would not be a blockade, as it had been in Grammie's house for a number of years and no one in the family had ever showed any interest in it.

The month of November was into its third week before Ann heard from Ira Harris. He made an appointment for her in the evening, as he knew she had to be on her job during the day. Ann took note of the date and was really looking forward to her allotted time with him, even though she was apprehensive about what he might have found.

Finally, the day arrived, and at seven o'clock that evening, Ann was in Mr. Harris' office. She sat across from him in anticipation of his findings. They had a few minutes of idle chit chat, and then he reached into his desk and removed some official-looking papers. He spread them out on his desk and hesitated before he started to talk.

"This was a very interesting search," he said. "It took some time to get this far, but I think I have accomplished what I needed to in order to make all of it yours. I searched the deed to the property first, and even though I hit a few snags in the road, I have all the claims to it cleared up, and it is officially yours.

"Your great-grandfather bought the land from a Milton Sullivan, who lived in the area. He has since passed away, and I had to check that no other member of his family had any claim to it. In my search, I found that Mr. Sullivan had some problems getting the land in his name, but after family ties to the property were solved, he was able to clear that up and the land was totally in his name when your great-grandfather bought it.

"As soon as you sign some papers, and we make a trip to the proper place, we will have it legally in your name. However, there is a problem before we do that, as the taxes on the property and the cabin have not been paid for a number of years. Considerable taxes are due before we can get it changed to your name. The question here is ... can you handle that?"

Ann heard everything he said and listened to his advice, but she'd never had anything to do with taxes and deeds before. Her father had looked after those things when she lived at home, and Grammie looked after her own. She would have to trust her lawyer.

"If I have to come up with some money to pay the back taxes," Ann said, "I am sure I can, unless it runs into thousands of dollars."

Mr. Harris shuffled through some papers and told her the amount. "The back taxes come to four thousand fifty-five dollars. Can you handle that amount of money?"

Ann thought for a few seconds and told him that she had some money saved and was sure she could get the remainder.

"Once the back taxes are paid, and we draw up a new deed in your name, the property will be yours. Now," he said, "there is the amount of the bank account. It stated specifically that the account was to go to the one who found the papers. There is no doubt that you found the papers. You were given the old violin by your grandmother. Your great-grandfather lived with your grandmother until his death and left his belongings with her. It was hers.

"He trusted her to give it to the right person, and apparently, she did. It definitely was to go to the first one who learned to play it, and that's you, Ann. The violin is yours and also the papers you found inside the lining of the case. Therefore, everything mentioned in those papers is yours. There is no way anyone can contest that. I have done many hours of research here and read about a number of such cases, and they all had the same result. If the deceased person stated they were to go to a certain person, then it was theirs.

"So, after a trip to the bank, where we will sign some papers, the account will be changed to your name. The bank would not tell me the amount of the funds in the account, so you will find out when it is turned over to you."

Ann sat there in complete silence. She could not believe she had all of a sudden become a land owner as well as the owner of a bank account with an unknown amount of funds. Perhaps it wouldn't be very much, but she didn't care. The fact that it was hers, and had been a gift from a famous great-grandfather she'd never known, was a joy to her. It made her more determined than ever to play the old violin to the very best of her ability.

"I am speechless," Ann told Mr. Harris. "I never in my wildest dreams imagined what might happen the day my grandmother told me I could have the violin. If you had seen it when I took it home with me, you would have wondered what I was ever going to do with that old broken-down piece of junk. Thank you so much for all your research and interest in my case. I really appreciate it."

He smiled. "I'll set up some appointments for you, one to visit the offices of the Municipality of Guysborough, in Guysborough, and the other with the Bank of Nova Scotia in Antigonish. I'll set them up during your Christmas break, as I know you have no other time available when these offices are open. I think that's all for now. So, I'll see you in the very near future."

Ann thanked him and left his office in anticipation of what all of this would mean or bring to her future, thinking about how life could throw you some surprises.

Ann went back to school on the first of December and was met with the same challenges. There were classes, problem students, good students, tests, and after school duties, all rolled into every day. She loved her job, but it was nice to look forward to the Christmas break coming up in a few weeks. She was also looking forward to the appointments being set up by her lawyer. It would be nice to have all of that straightened out and out of the way.

She could hardly believe that she would be the owner of a cabin and a strip of land, something she had never ever dreamed of. All of this put a little bit more anticipation and excitement into her days.

Christmas was always an exciting time for Ann. She loved buying gifts for her parents and her grandmother. She would go home for the holidays but would certainly find a day or two to spend with Grammie who would be anxious to hear what was happening with the papers she found and how she was getting along with making them legal.

Christmas Vacation

THE LAST SCHOOL DAY before Christmas vacation finally arrived, and Ann left the school with gifts some of her students had given her and some schoolwork she wanted to do over the holidays. She dropped them off at her house and went on to town to finish her Christmas shopping. She just had a few little things left to get for her parents and some peppermint patties she knew Grammie loved to have. She usually ate one before crawling into bed each night. It did not take long to finish and soon she was back at her house and preparing to leave for her parents' home for the Christmas holidays.

She arrived at her old home bearing gifts for her parents. She spent the rest of the day helping her mother with some Christmas baking and finishing trimming the tree.

Having completed these tasks, she put on her coat, hat, winter boots, and mittens, snapped the leash on Jake, the family dog (who was so glad to see her), and went out for a nice walk in the snow. The winter air was really quite cold and frosty, and the wind was very brisk but exhilarating.

Ann and Jake did a fast walk around the nearby school grounds and returned home. They were glad to get back, and the warmth of the house was inviting as they entered. Jake was glad to stretch out on a mat and get warm again. He was getting up in years and seemed to mind the cold now.

While she and her parents ate dinner that evening, she told them about the lawyer's findings and the appointments set up for her two days after Christmas. She also told them she would go over to Loch Broom and bring her grandmother over to their place for the holidays. They were glad she was able to do that for them as they still had much to do before Christmas Day, which was only two days away.

The next day, Ann went for Grammie and spent the night with her. They had a great chat about the lawyer's findings. Grammie was very interested in her story since she needed the end to Ann's story to finish her own write up on Alex Blair.

Grammie had done so much research on him that her story was almost a book. In fact, a publisher had asked her to write Alex Blair's story as they were interested in publishing it. Grammie told Ann she would love to have the story published in the form of a biography, but she was not sure her interpretation of his life was well enough presented for that to happen.

"Oh, Grammie, that is wonderful!" Ann almost shouted. "I'll read it and help you to amend anything that we feel can be put into better words. We can do that. Oh, I'm so happy for you!

"I know it was a great deal of work to put that together and had you not saved all those clippings of his years of playing, I'm sure it would have been very difficult for anyone to do research on his life and work. To have a publishing company want to publish the story for you is an honour. Take advantage of it. I'll help you. Oh, this is so exciting! My Grammie, the author!"

Once Christmas Day was over, Grammie went to work finishing her story, and that kept her busy for a couple of days. Ann had her meetings to attend and couldn't settle down to help Grammie until they were over.

She helped her mother clean up after Christmas dinner, putting the special-occasion dishes away, washing tablecloths and napkins, ironing them and then returning them to their rightful places. They'd had twelve folks for the big meal, and it required a great deal of work. They'd had a great time though, so it was well worth it. She got to see some aunts, uncles, and cousins she only saw once in a while and that made the work a pleasure.

Two days after Christmas found Ann back in Mr. Harris' office. Together, they went to the Office of Municipal District of Guysborough first, to register the deed of her great-grandfather's land and cabin in her name. The registrar looked the papers over and left with them to another office. Upon her return, she got Ann and Mr. Harris to sign them. She then put the seal of the county on the new deed, and the ownership was now in Ann's name. One job was completed.

Next, they drove to Antigonish. The day was beautiful. The sun was bright and produced diamonds in the fresh covering of snow that had fallen overnight. The road was plowed and the driving was excellent. Antigonish was about a twenty-five-minute drive from the town of Guysborough, and they were there on time for their appointment. Upon entering the bank, they were ushered to the right place and Mr. Harris explained that he had already been talking to the proper person and was there with Ann Blair to bring the situation to a close. They were left alone for a few minutes, and then a tall competent-looking lady entered. She carried a folder with some official looking papers in it.

"Good day," she said. "My name is Carol Murdoch."

They shook hands and she sat down behind a large desk. She shuffled the papers around and then said, "You're here to change the bank account of Alex Blair to his great-granddaughter, Ann Blair?"

"Yes, we are," answered Mr. Harris. "I've done all the preliminary work to have that accomplished. According to his instructions, Ann Blair is the rightful owner of the account. All the legal work has been done. Here are the legal papers. You may read them for yourself." He handed her the papers.

She took them and carefully read them. "It looks as though everything is in order, and there's no reason to not sign the account over to

Ann Blair. Do you have any identification on you, Ann? I should have your Social Insurance number."

Ann immediately produced her card and signed the proper papers. She now had the bank account in her name. She had it transferred to the bank of Nova Scotia in New Glasgow, because it was much closer to where she lived. The account had almost six hundred thousand dollars in it. To Ann, this was a fortune. On a teacher's salary, she didn't think she would ever be able to save that amount of money. Never in her wildest dreams did she ever feel she would have access to that amount of money.

Ann and Mr. Harris left the bank with Ann almost in a state of shock over her inheritance. Mr. Harris was pleased that he had successfully assisted her in achieving what was rightfully hers. Ann thanked her lawyer for all his help and told him to send his bill. He took Ann back to the village of Guysborough where she had left her car. Ann felt relieved and tired as she started her vehicle, let it warm up, and drove on to her parents' place.

The house felt warm and cozy as Ann entered it. She removed her winter boots and outer clothing and found her parents Bill and Barbara, (Ann's mother) and Grammie in the living room beside the fireplace. Jake was stretched out on a mat fast asleep. She told them all about her day's activities and how glad she was that everything had worked out successfully. They were very pleased for her.

"You look very tired, Ann," declared Grammie. "Why don't you take a nap? It will do you good."

Ann agreed with Grammie and made her way upstairs to her bedroom with Jake at her heels. She lay down on her bed, and Jake jumped up beside her. She pulled a comforter over herself, and Jake snuggled under it as well. Then they both were off to dream land.

Ann awoke with a start. She'd had a good sleep but she was sure she had been there much longer than she'd planned. She jumped up, folded the comforter, and placed it at the foot of the bed. Jake jumped down and trotted downstairs with her. She found Grammie having a little snooze in her chair by the fireplace, and her father was nowhere to be seen.

Things are really quiet around here, she thought, as she went to the door to let Jake out for a little run. She found her mom in the kitchen, so she went about helping her prepare the supper meal. She loved supper time when she was at home. They all sat around the table and talked after the meal. There were always some good stories that came to the surface and a whole lot of laughs. She often felt there were not enough times like this within families, and many of the old stories about the family were lost because of it.

They spent at least an hour bringing up things that happened over the years. Ann thought she might encourage Grammie to write some of them down and make a book of them. That would be a great keep-sake for all family members, and she was sure Grammie would like to do it. Grammie found the winters long, and it would give her some-thing to do that could be passed on to their future generations. She would discuss it with Grammie after she finished reading her write up on Alex Blair.

The next day was New Year's Day. Ann, her parents, and her grandmother ate a delicious diner prepared by Ann and her mother. They spent the remainder of the day relaxing. The following day, Ann was packing her things for her return to her house in Lawson Brook and preparing for school. Grammie was going to stay with her son and daughter-in-law for a while longer. She found the time long in the winter, when she couldn't get outside.

A New Year begins

CLASSES STARTED ON A Thursday of that week, and a noisy group of students, all excitedly telling each other what they got for Christmas, returned to classes. It would be a busy few weeks for them as midterm exams started the first of February. It took a day or two to get everyone back on track, but with the ever-important exams bearing down on them, it was soon down to serious studying. These marks were of utmost importance to the graduating class, as they were the marks used to give them entrance to their chosen university or trade school.

After exams were ended and all her marking and grading was finished, Ann found the time slipped by quickly. March Break and Easter came and went, and before she knew it, another school year had ended, and she was free for the months of July and August.

She spent the first two weeks of the summer vacation at her home doing some of the jobs she had neglected for the last few months of school. She managed to do some cleaning and shopping and put her house back in order. She was not a fussy housekeeper, but she did like to keep her house neat and tidy.

The big thing on Ann's mind now was the land and cabin. She had to make a trip to Guysborough to see her newly acquired asset. She talked it over with her father, and he agreed to go with her to find the land and the cabin of her great-grandfather—land that no one in the family knew anything about. Ann found this exciting and was looking forward to the trip.

Two days later, Ann and her father, Bill, were on their way to find her newly acquired cabin in the woods. Bill had been to that part of the province before and had a general idea of where the cabin was. He had the address given to Ann by Mr. Harris, so he felt finding it would not be too much of a problem. The directions her lawyer gave her were very good, and they had very little problem finding the cabin once they left the main highway near Boylston. They travelled a short distance on a rough country road and then turned up a driveway. After a steady climb, they came to another driveway that branched off theirs.

"There must be another cabin or house up here," Ann's father said. "I don't think Mr. Harris knew that or he would have told us."

"If we plan to spend any time here, I hope they'll be good neighbours," Ann said.

"I was wondering which one we should take, but there's a sign almost hidden by the bushes. Would you jump out and see what it says?" Bill asked.

Ann stepped out of the car, separated the greenery, and then the sign was quite clear: "A. Blair." She made her way back to the car, jumped in, and they were on their way again. They drove up a little farther, around a turn, and there it was, situated almost in the centre of an acre or more of cleared land. It was a beautiful white cabin with a deep red trim around the windows and doors. The cabin had a deck that went more than halfway around the building. It was painted the same deep red color as the trim. Ann could not believe her eyes. She hadn't expected to see anything as neat and tidy as this.

Her father was speechless. He'd had no idea as to what they would find when they started up the driveway, but it certainly wasn't what he was looking at. It had such a beautiful setting. There was a row of apple trees running perpendicular to the house and a piece of land that gave the appearance of having been used as a vegetable garden. There were shrub trees situated in spots that gave the property a semblance of continuity. The whole picture gave the viewer the sense that the one who planned the setting fully knew the presentation he wanted to create.

Ann and her father fell in love with the property even before they left the car. The view from up on the hill overlooking the Milford Haven River was as picturesque as one could imagine. Ann was wishing she had a chair or something to sit on so she could survey the vista for as long as she wanted. Never in her life had she seen another locale as breathtaking as this was.

Finally, she tore herself away from it, and she and her father entered the cabin. It was not as uplifting as the outside but was in fairly good repair. There was a reasonably good-sized kitchen, a large living room, a small dining room, two bedrooms, and a bathroom. They went out the back door and found there was a deck there as well. It was not as large as the front deck but would definitely be a great quiet spot to sit and read a good book.

The furnishings in each room were sparse and in need of replacement. It was barely livable as it was and could do with a complete overhaul. They didn't have time on this day to make a complete inspection of the repairs that must be made but decided to make another visit in the very near future to take note of all that had to be done.

They noted that the cabin was wired for electricity and there was a telephone there, but since they had not been used for some time, a complete inspection would have to be made and any rewiring would have to be tended to. However, in due time, they would make it a perfect "home away from home."

They might want to spend a Thanksgiving or Christmas there. They thought Grammie would really like that, but it needed some serious repairs before that could happen. They took one more walk through the cabin, which is when Ann saw a key on a window sill. She picked it up and put it in her pocket and then walked out the front door, locking it, and vowing they would be back very soon.

They left for home, but as they drove out the driveway, Ann told her father she was wondering what was up the other driveway that branched off theirs.

"There's only one way to find out," her father said.

When he reached the other driveway, he turned the car and made his way up to the top of it. When they had gone about as far as their cottage was off the main road, they reached another dwelling and were amazed at what they saw: a beautiful big house. It was a huge two-story mansion of a home, and appeared to be lived in year round, or at least most of the year.

The grounds were immaculate, with rolling lawns in every direction from the house. There were several rows of apple trees to the back of the house and beautiful flower gardens and shrubs that were neatly trimmed surrounding the front lawn and the two sides of the domain. There was a neatly trimmed privet hedge along the top half of the driveway.

Ann's father stopped the car, and the two of them sat there and gazed at the postcard picture before them. It was breathtaking. One would certainly not expect to see this lavish a home on the backroads of Guysborough County. Ann was wondering who this home could belong to.

She figured that, to have such a property, it had to be someone quite wealthy. The upkeep on it alone would cost a lot of money. Since they lived in close proximity to her measly little cottage, and practically on the same driveway, she knew it wouldn't take too long for her to find out. Her father turned the car and drove away before someone came out to see what they wanted.

They went down the road to a small restaurant and had some lunch. There were a number of customers present but no one paid any attention to them, which made Ann think they weren't from the area either. Following lunch, they drove around the area for an hour or so and then went on home and spent some time telling Ann's mother, Barbara, all about the cabin and the other house almost on the same driveway.

The day after her trip to the cabin, Ann went over to visit her grand-mother. Grammie was really interested in the whereabouts of the cabin and the shape it was in. Ann told her about the day she and her father had spent there, and also about the other gorgeous property next door. She also told her about the bank account and the amount of money that had been left to her.

She explained that she was going to use some of the money to fix up the cabin and make it a cozy, comfortable place for a summer home for her parents, her grandmother, and herself. She also told her that she was going to give some of the money to her parents, her aunt Mary (Bill's sister), and Grammie.

Her first priority though was to make the cabin a good home away from home. She would divide the remainder of the money after that, keeping a portion of it for the upkeep of the cabin and property. She and Grammie talked for a long time, and it was soon long past their bedtime. Grammie went to bed with the feeling that she could now finish the last part of her write up on Ann's great-grandfather.

Ann stayed with Grammie for most of the next day and helped her with her write up. As she read it through, she found out some interest-ing things her great-grandfather had done throughout his life. He was a very talented and interesting person, having travelled to many parts of the world with his music. He married and had two children, her granduncle, Herbert Blair, and grandfather, George, who was married to her grandmother, the former Annie Fraser, better known now as "Grammie," at least to her. Herbert was a lawyer in New Glasgow and married Alice Nelson. Grammie and George had two children, Ann's father William and her aunt Mary.

Grammie had done a fairly good job of her story. Except for some grammatical errors and the odd misspelling here and there, Ann thought Grammie had done a good life story on her great-grandfather. She typed it for Grammie and prepared it for mailing. It would be interesting to see what happened to Grammie's version of the life of the great Alex Blair.

Ann did some other small tasks Grammie felt might be a bit danger-ous for her to do, especially alone. Climbing up ladders or on chairs to reach high places that needed cleaning was left for a family visitor. Ann never minded helping in this way. As soon as she had completed the necessary jobs, Grammie wanted done, Ann packed her things, said goodbye to Grammie, gave her a hug, and left for her parents' place. She still had a few weeks of vacation left before school started.

Ann couldn't get the cabin out of her mind. She talked it over with her father. He found a good carpenter in the area, and they scheduled a time to go back to the cabin with him. There was a great amount of repair work to be done, and Ann's father felt many of them should be completed before the cold weather set in. As for Ann, she wanted to get them done as soon as possible. She had visions of, perhaps, spending Christmas there.

The carpenter met Ann and her father at the cabin at the allotted time. They spent hours there going over the repairs that needed to be done. They decided the outside repairs needed to be looked after before any work would be done inside. The carpenter, Jim Austen, was very thorough in his perusal of the outside repairs and came up with a list of things the cabin needed in order to put it in good shape and make it look the way he was sure Ann wanted.

Mr. Austen gave her an account of items needing repairs and another of things that had never been there in the first place. The cabin needed a foundation. Presently it was just sitting on concrete blocks, and some of those were about to slide out of place. There was a bathroom in the house, but the septic system was in need of replacing. The roof needed new shingles and the sides of the cabin had a number of rotting boards, so the siding had to be restored. It was in bad need of new windows and doors, and the decks (both back and front) were not very safe as they were. In short, it needed a considerable amount of work.

Mr. Austen handed the list to Ann and her father. He told them they might want to consider tearing it down and just building a new cabin in its place. Ann immediately vetoed that suggestion. She felt she wanted to keep the main part of the cabin the way it was and just do whatever repairs were necessary. It was something her great-grandfather had left behind for her, although he didn't know exactly who would fall heir to it.

Since she was that person, she was going to keep as much of it as possible. The main part of the cabin would stay as he had left it. She took the list and decided she would talk it over with her father before she made any decisions. She asked if he was available to do the job right away, and he said that he had one small job to finish but that it would take less than a week to do so. Following that, he would be able to do the work. They left it at that, and he departed.

Bill and Ann stayed a while longer and discussed what he had recommended. He was right on all the outside work that needed to be replaced. They both agreed on that. However, Ann had another idea.

"Dad," she said, "I've been thinking that I'd like to lift the cabin up and put a foundation and a basement under it. I'd also like to enlarge the dining room and kitchen and add another bedroom and bathroom. That would mean adding a piece to the existing building. Could that be done?"

"Certainly," Bill said. "It would cost a great deal more money but would surely be a nice addition to the cabin, which would no longer be a cabin but a nice house. Are you sure you want to do that?"

"I would like this house to be a nice comfortable place for the family. I know I got what my great-grandfather left, but I can share it with the rest of the family in that way. Let's go home and consider it. You're very good at this type of thing. I'm sure you can draw it up for me."

They drove home, sat down at the kitchen table, and discussed what Jim Austen had said and the list he'd given them of his recommendations. They came to the conclusion that he was correct in all of them.

Everything that he said had to be done would be done, and hopefully right away.

The conversation then switched to the changes Ann wanted to make. They drew a sketch of the inside of the cabin as it was now. Bill was quite good at this. He drew the addition Ann suggested and felt it would be easy enough to do. Another bedroom and an extra bathroom, along with making the dining room and kitchen larger, would be a real asset to the structure.

It would be a large enough annex to make the bathroom big enough to include a washer and dryer. Ann figured that placing them in the basement would mean a lot of carrying clothes up and down stairs, and as they got older, that would become more of a chore. She was thinking of her parents here. They would not always be as young and vibrant as they now were. Even her energy would wane as the years passed, so placing them upstairs was good thinking.

The extra bedroom would give rooms for her parents, Grammie, and herself should they all wish to come at the same time, and it was likely that they would. She let Bill derive a plan for the addition, and when they met with Mr. Austen later in the week, they would get his approval or make any changes he thought would enhance their new home away from home.

They met with Jim Austen a few days later. He carefully reviewed the plan Bill had drawn up and said that he thought it was feasible. He would do his best to do as they wished and would be ready to start right away. They discussed the business end of the deal and came to an agreement that suited both of them. The job was ready to start.

Ann would have to depend on her father to take charge as she was back to school in a few days. Bill was retired, so it was possible for him to see that things were going ahead as planned.

Back at school, Ann was very excited to come back to the cabin every weekend to see the progress that had been made. The cabin was raised and the basement was dug, including the space for the new addition. The concrete foundation was poured, and the cabin was set back on the new basement walls.

The floor for the basement was also poured and was ready to be walked on the first time Ann was able to come back. It was an exciting time for her as she watched the changes take place. It was no longer a cabin. It was a gorgeous cottage, and the view from above the river seemed more beautiful each time she viewed it.

Near the end of October, the outside work was almost complete. The roof was shingled, and the sides of the house were a nice yellow with brown gable ends and white trim around the doors and windows. Two new storm doors and outside doors were in place and new windows installed. The decks were replaced and trimmed in white. The deck floors were done in pretreated lumber and left unpainted. It was a very nice job, and Mr. Austen was rightfully proud of what he had accomplished to that point.

The inside was next, and again, Ann and her father sat down to do some planning. They talked about the changes they wanted for each room in the house. Oak trim was a must for every room. All outside walls were to be insulated and plastered and then painted. The chimney and fireplace had already been done, so that was fine, but the bathrooms and kitchen were to have new oak cabinets. They made every effort to see that there would be no doubts as to what was wanted. They drew up a list of requirements for each room and then made an appointment with Jim Austen. They met at the appointed time and went over the list with him. He said he would do his best to do as they wished, and that if he had any questions, he would contact them.

Ann and her father left Jim to do his job. They went on to get Barbara and then on to Halifax to select tubs, toilets, sinks, showers, and taps for the two bathrooms. They also needed a sink for the kitchen and light fixtures for the entire house, inside and out. It was a busy day, and they returned completely exhausted but feeling good with all they had accomplished during the day.

The job progressed nicely. As time went on, there were a number of other things that needed to be purchased, but Ann was so busy with her schoolwork that she left those to her father. She made a trip home each weekend to keep up on the progress being made on her project in Guysborough. Things were really taking shape, and with each visit, she was more pleased with the job Jim Austen and his workers were doing. Perfection seemed to be their aim, and they were achieving it.

They were into the month of December now, and it was clear that things were not going to be ready for this Christmas, but there was always next year. It was costing a great deal of money to make the cabin into a gorgeous cottage, but the money was left to her and that is what she wanted to do with it. She felt her great-grandfather would be pleased that the cabin had not been torn down but turned into a beautiful home.

Christmas saw the completion of the renovations. The last to be finished was the kitchen, where oak cupboards were installed, including one designed as an island near the centre of the kitchen, which could be used by the family for breakfasts and sometimes lunch. Four stools were added to complete the setting. All floors were oak, with the exception of the kitchen and bathrooms. These were done in ceramic tile. The stove, refrigerator, and dishwasher were hooked up and ready for use. As far as Jim Austin and crew were concerned, the job was complete.

While the construction work was being done, Ann and her mother had made many trips to Antigonish, New Glasgow, and Halifax on weekends, in search of new furniture for three bedrooms, the dining room, living room, and kitchen. All the other essentials for the new home were purchased, and Ann and her mother spent Christmas vacation and a good part of the winter situating furniture, making beds, and setting up the kitchen with the necessary items so they wouldn't have to bring any supplies with them when they visited, except for food.

The house was finally set up as they wanted, except for one thing, as far as Ann was concerned. To her it needed just one more thing. There was a piano in Ann's parent's house and it was seldom played. Ann asked Bill and Barbara if it would be possible to move it to their new second home in Guysborough. Barbara thought about it for a few minutes and she and Bill agreed it would be a nice spot for the instrument and it would probably get more use there than at their home. There was an excellent spot for it in the living room and Ann, Bill, and Barbara were pleased as they stood and surveyed their new home away from home. Easter was later this year, so when it arrived, their plan was to take Grannie up to see the "old cabin" (as she referred to it) for the first time and have their Easter dinner there. The house was finished and everything was in place. In fact, it was beautiful. It now was a home anyone would be happy to own and enjoy.

Ann was very pleased and happy with her decision to make it into a nice home. As soon as spring arrived, she knew her father would be there working on the grounds. He had a knack for that type of work, and she knew he would know exactly what to do to make it the best it could be.

Gardening and the positioning of shrubs and trees were no challenge to him, and he had the ability to envision the end product at the beginning. Ann had no doubt that he could make the grounds picture perfect.

Chapter 10

Home Away from Home

EASTER FINALLY ARRIVED, AND it was time to take Grammie up to the house they had spent a good part of the previous year working on. Grammie was back with Bill and Barbara for the winter months, and she and Ann followed Bill and Barbara to the new house in Guysborough. Grammie had not been down this way for a very long time, and she really enjoyed the drive. She was amazed at the changes that had taken place since the last time she had been in this part of the province.

The main difference to her was the fact that they almost bypassed New Glasgow and Antigonish to make the trip. The last time she had been in the area, which was a good few years past, one would drive through both towns. They turned off the main highway at Monastery and on to Boylston. Then they veered off the main road to Canso onto the North Riverside Road.

They went a short distance and then turned up an unpaved road. About a mile up that road, they turned into a driveway that seemed to be climbing continually; then it split and they continued to the left, up a short distance, around a turn, and there was their new Guysborough residence.

Grammie thought they were headed into the woods never to be seen again. She couldn't believe what she was seeing as they approached the doorway of this beautiful home in the "back woods," as she referred to it.

"Oh, my goodness, I didn't expect to see something as nice as this. I thought you folks told me it was a cabin. This is a gorgeous house. This is a long way from what you described to me when you first saw it."

"It is a long way from when I first saw it," Ann said. "We did a great deal of work on it."

"Just think what this place will look like when your father gets to work on it in the spring! Your great-grandfather would be so happy and proud if he could see it now," Grammie said.

Then she frowned, deep in thought. "I wonder why he strayed away up here to build this shelter in the woods? Did he have a reason to build here? I've often wondered about that. As far as I know, there has never been a Blair in this part of the province, at least not from this Blair family. It seems very strange to me."

They got out of their cars and went into the house. The place was quite chilly, so Bill turned the furnace up and went to light the fireplace in the living room. He told Grammie to keep her coat on until the house was warmer. Ann removed her coat, as she was wearing a big sweater, made sure Grammie had her slippers on, and took her on a tour around the house.

Grammie was awestruck. She knew they had done quite a lot of work on the cabin, but she had never expected this. This was one of the nicest homes she had ever been in. She loved it, and the fact that it was all on the same floor, with the exception of the basement, was a big plus as far as she was concerned. She felt she would never have any reason to go to the basement anyway.

The house was quite warm by the time Grammie finished the tour, so she took her coat off and sat in a rocker beside the fireplace. Ann brought her some tea.

They spent the whole Easter weekend up on the hill overlooking the beautiful Milford Haven River. With Ann's assistance, Barbara cooked a nice dinner of ham with all the trimmings, and they thoroughly enjoyed their first meal in Guysborough County. They spent the remainder of the weekend enjoying the house and the area.

THE TIME TO GO home came too soon, but all good things come to an end. The next day, Ann was back at her desk, and the busiest part of the school year began. She found herself in the midst of planning, so she would be sure to finish all the required lessons for the completion of another school year. There were also extracurricular activities she was involved with, and those took up a great amount of her time.

She made sure she did not give up any time for her violin lessons and practice time. Her talent for the violin was really beginning to show, and she certainly did not want to sacrifice any time involved with that. She was a very busy person but somehow managed to get time for all of it. It took planning and sacrifice, but she was up to the challenge, and besides, summer was coming and she could find time for relaxation then. Right now, there was work to do.

As always, the school year ended, and after remaining at her own home for a week or so to do some tasks she had been neglecting over the past weeks, she packed some things and drove to her parents' place. She spent a couple days with them and then drove over to Loch Broom to see Grammie. They spent a delightful evening talking about her job, the newly acquired house she now owned in Guysborough, and what she planned to do for the summer months. As the clock struck eleven, they both decided to call it a day and retired.

Ann was up bright and early the next morning. She didn't make her usual visit to the river. Instead, she helped Grammie make breakfast and did some chores that needed to be done. She helped Grammie with the laundry and did some baking for her. She worked well into the afternoon, helping Grammie with a few of the things that now gave her a bit of a problem when she tackled them on her own. Having finished these, Ann took Grammie with her and drove to her own place, to make sure everything was fine there, and then drove on to her new home in Guysborough.

Ann and her parents spent a great part of the summer at her new house. Bill was very busy with the grounds, and things were taking shape. It might not be as elaborate as their neighbour's property, but it was well planned, with red maple trees and a privet hedge along the driveway. The lawns were smooth, and the grass was a rich green, encouraging people to kick off their shoes and go barefoot.

Bill had placed flower gardens and shrubs in strategic spots, and as the summer progressed, the grounds took on the appearance of a perfectly beautiful property. Bill was proud of his achievement, and Ann could not have been happier with the results.

On one of her mornings in Guysborough, Ann decided she would like to go down to the river she could see so well from her house. She was a little afraid of walking the lonesome road all alone, so she drove down most of the way, parked her car by the side of the road, and then walked down to the sandy beach.

It was beautiful and inviting, and as the sun started its daily trip up into the sky, Ann did what she usually did. She sat on the sand and took off her sandals. The time passed as she watched eagles soar over the river. She was surprised to see one take a dive toward the water and come up with a wriggling fish. Then it flew off into the distance to enjoy its breakfast. Ann figured that eagle's day was off to a good start.

She decided she had better go home or her parents would be wondering where she was. She slipped on her sandals and was just about to stand up when she was startled to see someone standing beside her.

"Why, hello there!" he said. "I see someone else likes to come here as much as I do."

Ann looked up at the seemingly friendly gentleman.

"Hello," she answered. "You startled me. I didn't see you coming."

"I usually walk down here every morning," he said. "It gets my day off to a good start."

"I was a little nervous to come all the way by myself, so I drove down from my place. It overlooks this river. I know it sounds a bit lazy, but I'm not very familiar with the area. Perhaps, as time goes on, I'll become braver. You make this walk every day?"

"Pretty much. It starts my day off with some good exercise. It's not too difficult a walk down here from my place, but it is quite a climb back up."

"So you live near here?"

"Well, it is quite a little hike," he said. "I live up off the Old Guysborough Road. My house overlooks this river too. I love it up there. It just seems like I'm looking down on the rest of the world."

She nodded. "I love walking first thing in the morning too. Maybe, when I get used to the place, I'll walk all the way to the river too. It's so beautiful here. It's so nice to sit on the sand and forget about every-thing and just enjoy what you're seeing."

"Aha," he said. "A girl after my own heart. I like that. So, you live in the area," he said "I've never seen you."

"I'm new here, but yes, I do. Well, at least for parts of the year, and your place sounds a lot like mine. My great-grandfather left me a cabin overlooking the river, and I made it into a house last summer and fin-ished it during the winter."

The gentleman looked surprised and stared at her for a few seconds.

"Ah… so then you're one of the folks with the driveway that my drive-way branches off. This is a nice surprise. I really wanted to meet the people who lived so close to me. I just didn't want to be a nosy neigh-bour and go prying into what you were doing. And I never had the opportunity to see you anywhere - at least, not that I know of."

"Wow!" exclaimed Ann. "This is my lucky day. We wondered who lived up your driveway but didn't have the opportunity to meet you folks either. This is so nice. I'm Ann… Ann Blair. I own the house almost beside yours. I'm so glad to finally meet you."

"Why hello, Ann Blair. I'm Shane Robertson, your next-door neighbour."

"Have you always lived here?" Ann asked.

"No. My parents and I built our house here a few years back. I'm not always here, so when I leave, Mom and Dad stay in the house. They love it here. They're retired, so it gives them a place for a change of scenery."

Ann jumped up. "I have to get back to the house. Would you like a drive?"

"Yes, actually. I'm a little behind in my schedule today, and I have something I have to finish. My deadline is close."

"Oh dear," Ann said. "What are you doing that's so crucial? It sounds really important."

"As soon as we get to my place, why don't you come in for a cup of coffee, and I'll fill you in."

"Sounds interesting. I'll do that," Ann answered.

They drove to the beautiful house and property Ann recalled sneaking a peek at with her father. It was as gorgeous as she remembered.

"You have a really nice place here," Ann told him.

"Well, it's not totally mine. I own it with my parents. They travel a great deal of the time, so I get to spend much of my time here. I'm a writer, and it gives me a quiet place to write and not be disturbed. I know very few people here, so I don't have many visitors. The cabin was always a mystery to us, as we had no idea who owned it, and there never seemed to be anyone there. It was a surprise when all of a sudden there were bulldozers, well drillers, and delivery trucks going up and down the driveway."

Ann then told him the story of how she'd become heir to the property and how there was enough money left to make a real home out of it, so she'd felt obliged to do so.

"Wow!" he said when she finished her story. "I could write a good book on that. Oh, don't look so startled, I would never do that without your permission."

"Have you published many books?"

"Yes, quite a few, mostly novels. I always have my ears open for a happening I can turn into a factious tale. I have a Masters in English from Dalhousie University. I wasn't sure where to go from there. I thought about teaching, but I felt I really didn't have the patience for that. I'm a little bit of a loner, and writing serves me well in that department. I think I made the right choice. I have been successful thus far, and I love what I do. But that's enough about me. What do you do?"

"I'm in the profession you turned down. I guess I have the patience, and I love to be among people, especially young people. I teach high-school mathematics, and I love what I do. It has always been my dream to be a teacher. It is a tough job sometimes but a very rewarding one."

He got up to make more coffee, and Ann watched him as he worked over the coffee maker. She realized he was a handsome man. He was about five foot eleven with short, wavy brown hair, deep blue eyes, beautiful teeth, and the lopsided grin of a young mischievous boy. Ann always noticed a person's hands, and he had the hands of a professional person, with long slim fingers resembling those of a musician. If she were to describe him to someone else, she would have to admit he was well worth a second look. Not only that, he seemed a very nice and extremely intelligent individual.

The coffee was ready, and she enjoyed a second cup with him as they continued to get to know each other. They forgot all about the time, until finally, Ann said she had to go, reminding him that he had work to do, which he had been so adamant about a few hours ago.

He admitted that he probably should have been working but would not have traded the few hours they had spent getting to know each other for any amount of work. He really liked Ann and was looking forward to future encounters. He walked her to her car.

"Would you like to come for coffee some time?" Ann asked, as she got into her car. "Or maybe lunch?"

"Yes, I would. It would be nice to continue our conversation. We'll likely meet at the river again. If you'd like to walk down and would feel more comfortable with company, just give me a call. I'd love to have some company myself."

They exchanged phone numbers, and Ann left for her house. She felt she had just enjoyed a nice morning and was looking forward to more of the same. When she returned home, her father was mowing the lawns and her mother was busy in the flower gardens. Both of them loved working outside, and this summer, both spent most of their time enjoying the outdoors. Ann joined her mother in the flower gardens, and as they worked away, Ann told her all about her encounter with Shane and how they had talked about some of the things that had happened in both their lives. She said she found him very interesting and easy to talk with.

The next morning, Ann was up bright and early. Her parents had still not appeared on the scene when she got a phone call from Shane, asking if she was going for her walk to the riverside. He said that, if she was, he would meet her at the divide in the driveway. She told him she would like that and left a note for her parents. Then she walked to the split in the driveway and found Shane waiting for her. They walked out of the driveway and down the hill, talking all the way. They had very little trouble finding things to discuss, and in doing so, got to know each other better.

Ann found she really liked Shane. He was obviously very knowledgeable on a number of subjects but made no special attempt to make her aware of that. Through their conversations, she realized he had travelled a great deal. When he wrote a novel in which he had to describe certain places, he visited that locale, no matter where it was in the world, and was able to get the feeling of it. That was the only true way he could effectively depict the place and situation he was writing about.

Ann had never done much travelling, so she listened intently as he told her of some of the countries he had spent time in. It forced her to make a promise to herself that she would do some visiting in other countries. She would love to find out how other people lived and made their living. She wanted to see the countryside and walk in their shoes for a little while.

Shane listened to Ann as she told him about her childhood, and her days at school and university. He loved hearing stories of her teaching and some of the funny things that happen when one is working with teenagers. It reminded him of when he was a teenager himself.

He had not exactly been a teacher's joy to have in the classroom. He was a bit of a "little devil." He was not a troublesome student, just a jokester and the one who could sometimes make, or spoil, a well-prepared lesson. Probably, some of his antics made for a good laugh when they were told in the staffroom but were not so humorous at the time it happened. Later on, when Ann got time to read some of his books, she would find out that a little bit of his true character came out in his writing.

Again, they sat and talked for a few hours and they still had to climb back up the hill. They talked all the way back and parted with the promise to meet again in a day or two. Shane asked Ann if she had a bicycle, and she said she did, but it was at her home. She promised she would bring it with her the next time she visited.

"That would be great. We can bike around the countryside and perhaps have lunch at that restaurant in Guysborough. I think it is called 'Happy Days'. I heard it's very good."

"I would like that," declared Ann. "I've not been on my bike since last summer. That would give me a chance to get going on it again. I'd love to go for a bike ride."

They parted company and Ann walked up the driveway, eventually settling on her deck and looking out over the river she had just visited. It seemed so lazy and serene, just as it did when she sat beside it on the sand. The eagles were still soaring around and feeding on the fish below. It was nature at its best and was a picture to be enjoyed to its fullest.

After a while, her father joined her and they sat there talking for a period of time, discussing her morning and her talks with Shane. She told him they were going to do some bike riding around the area soon, and her father just smiled. Then he got up and went into the house for a short rest. He had been busy mowing the lawns and trimming some of the shrubs and small trees he had planted. The property looked great, but it took a huge amount of work to keep it looking that way.

Grammie's Surprise

ANN WAS HAVING A great time at her new home in Guysborough. However, she thought she'd better go home for a day and check on things there. She drove to Lawson Brook and found that all was fine there. She was going to spend the night at home before going on to Grammie's the next morning but changed her mind. She had a feeling that Grammie might want her to visit right away. It wasn't a panicky feeling, just a kind of a sensation that there was something she should know.

She drove down her grandmother's driveway and parked the car in front of the house. Grammie was at the door almost before Ann was. She was all excited.

Ann wondered what was on her mind. Grammie was waving an envelope in front of her face.

"Oh Ann, I am so glad to see you! Look at what came in the mail today!"

Grammie opened the envelope and pulled out a sheet of paper. She had received a letter back about the life story she had written on Alex Blair. It thanked her for her efforts and then the letter informed her that a movie company wanted to make a film of Alex Blair's life story, and they wanted her permission to do so. Grammie was so excited she could hardly contain herself. She could not believe she had written something that was good enough for a movie.

Ann took the letter from her and reread it. She was almost as taken back as her grandmother. This was good news. Grammie was right. Alex Blair was a truly great violinist who had played all over the world and had never received the honours he deserved. This was *great* news.

The letter also stated that Grammie was to receive a large sum of money for her endeavour, and asked if there was anyone in the family who played the violin. If there was, it asked if that person would be willing to do so in the movie. It would not be a leading role but an important one, as that person would represent the Blair family in the movie and would play the piece of music, written by Alex Blair, that had been found in the case, which was called "The Old Violin"

Ann stood there with the letter in her hand and read it again. There was only one person in the family who played the violin, and that was Ann herself—at least, she had never heard of anyone else.

"The only person in the family who plays the violin is you, Ann," exclaimed Grammie. "You would be the perfect person for that role."

Ann sat down. This was a lot to take in. She just came over to take Grammie back with her to Guysborough, and now she was being asked to take part in a film. This was a lot to handle in such a short period of time. It suddenly seemed that her quiet, peaceful life had taken a turn, a sharp turn, and she did not know if she was prepared for that. She decided to let it sink in first. She would just sleep on it and see how she felt in the morning.

Grammie and Ann prepared some supper, sat out on the deck, and ate it as they discussed the letter and its contents. Grammie said that she had not been expecting this result when she wrote all she could remember and found the many clippings she had saved over the years. Most of those clippings had been given to her by her sister-in-law, Herbert Blair's wife, Alice, who had passed away a few years before.

"What do you think, Ann? If this goes ahead, and it looks as though it will, would you be willing to take the part?" asked Grammie.

"I would have to put some real thought into that one," answered Ann. "I have a job I must get back to in a few weeks. I'd need a leave of absence to be able to do it. Of course, that would all depend on when they plan to film it. Perhaps it's not going to happen for some time. I guess I'll just cross that bridge when it happens."

Grammie had a bottle of red wine someone had given her. She produced the wine and two goblets. She poured some for Ann and some for herself, and they had a drink to celebrate. This was the first time in her life Grammie had won any acclaim for something she had done. She was going to bask in the moment with her favourite granddaughter.

As they sat, talked, and enjoyed their wine, Ann told her all about the great job her father had done on the lawns at the house in Guysborough. As soon as they finished their wine, she helped Grammie pack a few things so they could leave first thing in the morning. Ann was anxious to show Grammie the property, since she had not seen the finished product. They went to bed, were up early in the morning, and drove off to the house in Guysborough. They ate breakfast in Antigonish, on the way down, and arrived at their destination around ten o'clock.

"That looks great!" exclaimed Grammie as they drove up to the house. "I'm impressed. I didn't realize my son was so talented at this type of work. The place looks so nice. If your great-grandfather could see this, he would know the right person got his property."

Bill and Barbara came out of the house when they heard the car pull up. When Grammie and Ann got out of the car, they walked Grammie around the grounds and then up onto the front deck, where they could see the eagles circle over the river in search for food, while Ann went into the house. She returned with glasses of lemonade and some of Barbara's oatcake that were just fresh out of the oven.

They spent some time on the deck just catching up on the news. It was a beautiful day and the temperature was just right for enjoying the outside. Ann told her parents all about the letter Grammie had received about her written report on the life of Alex Blair.

Grammie had the letter with her. She took it out of her purse and handed it to Bill. He read it, said nothing, and gave it to Barbara. She also read it and said nothing. Ann and Grammie looked at each other in surprise.

"Is there something wrong?" Ann asked.

"Nothing," Bill said. "There's nothing wrong. We're just surprised. I guess I didn't realize Alex Blair, my grandfather, was such an important figure in the music world, but then again, I've never given it much thought. He did play throughout the world as part of some great orchestras. He even played at concerts on his own, and those concerts were well attended. Perhaps we in the family had no idea how important a figure he was. The only thing that bothered me was why he left the music world so suddenly, and all at once, disappeared.

"We often wondered why he did that and where he went. Now that Ann has found the papers in his old violin case, we know where he went, but we still don't know why." Bill shrugged. "Well, maybe time will tell us that too. Perhaps you should have another look in the old case, Ann. Maybe there's more information there. Who knows? He might have had some more secrets we're not aware of. Perhaps we should do some more digging."

Ann and Grammie were still dismayed. They'd expected a little more of a to-do than what they had received. Granted, there were still some missing pieces in the life story of her great-grandfather, but did her parents know something they were not telling her or were they just surprised that Grammie had done such a good write up of his life that it was worthy of letting the world know about his accomplishments?

Ann had the feeling there was a bit of mystery here, and it triggered a desire within her to find out what was missing. It might take some time, but she was determined that, if there was more to the story, she would find it.

The next morning, Ann was up early. She called Shane to see if he was going to walk to the river. He told her he was just leaving and would meet her at the juncture in the driveway. Ann donned her walking shoes, grabbed a cap, and struck off down the driveway. They met, exchanged salutations, and walked off together, out of the driveway and down the road to the river.

They stood for a few minutes just to enjoy the scenery, and then sat on the sand and once again watched the eagles catching fish from the river below. How happy and free from worry their lives appeared as they carried off squirming fish to the edge of the river and enjoyed their breakfast.

Ann looked at Shane and then back at the water. She was sometimes amazed at how easy it was for them to feel so comfortable with each other. They could sit on the shore and not say very much. They found it very enjoyable to just relish their time together, or they could talk for hours and never run out of things to discuss. He seemed like someone she had known all her life, yet she had only met him a short time ago.

Once a couple hours had passed, they decided to make the return trip back up to their respective homes before someone came looking for them. The trek back up was not as easy as the one down, but all too soon, they were back to the split in the driveway and they had to part.

When they were about to leave each other, Shane asked Ann if she had remembered her bicycle when she was home. She told him she had and that her father had checked it over to make sure it was in good working order.

"I've some work I have to do tomorrow, but the next day, maybe we could go touring around the area and view some of the sights?"

"Oh, I'd love to do that. I haven't seen much of the area and that would be a good chance to do just that."

They parted company, and Ann made her way up the remainder of the driveway, sat on one of the chairs on the deck, and looked at the river from above. One could get a different perspective of it from up here. However, to Ann it was beautiful regardless of which angle or altitude it was surveyed from.

Ann sat there for some time just thinking about Shane. He seemed like someone she had always known. He had so many characteristics that were familiar to her. One thing that really stood out was the fact that he was left-handed. Her father was left-handed, though it wasn't prevalent in the Blair family. In fact, it was very rare. She couldn't think of any other member of the family who was left handed.

Shane also had the deepest blue eyes. Her father had deep blue eyes. Their eyes were so much alike, and with both of them, when they looked at you, it was sometimes impossible to decide if they were laughing with you or at you.

Oh well, thought Ann, *lots of people are left-handed and have deep blue eyes.* She put the thought out of her mind, got up, and went into the house.

Grammie was at the kitchen table peeling apples, and Barbara was busy making an apple pie. There was a lemon pie already cooling on the counter, along with a batch of biscuits and a cookie can filled with fresh chocolate-chip cookies. The kitchen smelled like a bake shop.

Ann made a cup of coffee and slipped a couple cookies out of the can. As soon as the apple pie was in the oven, the three of them sat and chatted for some time. Then Grammie said she thought she would lie down for a short nap, and Barbara went out to see what Bill was doing. Ann took this time to do some laundry and tidy her bedroom.

Later in the afternoon, Ann took the letter Grammie had received and read it over again. As she did so, she wished she had the write up Grammie had done on her great-grandfather. She felt there might be something in it that would give a clue to the mystery that seemed to be attached to his life story.

It did seem strange that he had suddenly left the music industry and disappeared, not being heard from again until he appeared at his son George's home, years later, with just a few belongings, including his old violin. He was buried in the family plot in Alma beside his wife and parents. This part of his life was well known, and they now knew he spent at least some of those missing years hiding in a cabin in Guysborough. Why did he pick this area to build a cabin and what seemed to drive him here? Was there some attraction other than the beautiful river view?

Ann sat on the front deck for some time, pondering these questions. There was some reason for his disappearance from the music world.

His family had already grown up. He only had the two sons: George, Bill's father, and Herbert. His wife, Mary, Ann's great-grandmother, had passed away from cancer in her early sixties, and that had left him alone, but he still had his music. That was always one of the mainstays of his life.

But why did he leave it at a time when he needed it most? There had to be a reason, and Ann was determined to find out what it was. Music was his calling, and someone as dedicated as he was did not just up and leave it to live alone in a cabin on a hill overlooking a river … especially one that he had, probably, never seen before in his lifetime. Ann was convinced there was more to his story.

The remainder of the summer went too fast for Ann. She spent a good amount of her time touring around the Guysborough area with Shane on their bicycles. They rode all along the eastern shoreline of the county and walked miles in the sand. They pedaled down to the village of Canso and ate at a restaurant there. A fisherman from the area gave them a sail through the small islands just off the coast of Canso. They visited Hazel Hill, where one of the first transatlantic cables came across from Europe to North American.

They visited Dover, which seemed small but fairly well populated. The homes were small and most people seemed to fish for a living. On one time out, they were starting to get tired but had continued on to Guysborough, where they stopped at Happy Days restaurant for a meal and a rest.

Ann was pleased with her days. She got some exercise on her

bicycle, ate some good food, and could not have had anyone better to be with. They were very compatible and talked continually. They seemed to have the same sense of adventure and were almost two of a kind. Ann wasn't sure if she felt any romantic interest in him, but if not, he was a great friend.

On the last week of August, Shane came to say goodbye to her as he had some meetings with his publisher and then was making a trip to Australia to get some information for the next novel he was writing.

They shared a cup of coffee and some of Barbara's good cinnamon rolls. Ann walked him to his car, gave him a hug, and then watched as he drove down the driveway. There was something about him that was as familiar as a member of her family; however, those feelings were starting to change.

THE NEXT DAY, ANN and Grammie left Guysborough for home. For Ann, it was back to reality as well. She unloaded some things at home, took Grammie to dinner at Skipper's Landing in Lawson Brook, and then on to her house in Loch Broom. She made sure Grammie was settled back at home and then continued on to her own home. She retired early for a good night's sleep.

A Busy Year

THE FIRST OF SEPTEMBER found Ann back at school and ready for the coming year. Her grade-ten classes were large, and her workload was heavier than usual. The first month was the usual hassle of getting classes settled and getting to know her students. One of her first priorities was to be able to put a name to all her students by the end of the first month. She always found she had a better relationship with them if she was able to know them all by name as soon as possible. Gradually things settled down, and the school year was underway.

The first week of October, she had her first music lesson with Elsa Smith. She had played some over the summer and was glad to get back into a routine. She loved playing. It took her mind away from the regular practices of everyday life. She was becoming a very good violinist, and Elsa Smith told her she was soon going to have to get someone with more knowledge than she had, as Ann was very gifted. If she wished to continue, it was something they had to consider.

Thanksgiving weekend could not come quick enough as Ann found herself swamped with schoolwork. She was up many nights well past midnight preparing lessons and marking papers. She also had house-work and shopping, and wanted to keep up with her violin lessons. Life was very busy, and the very thought of a day or two away from all of that was something to look forward to.

She started the Thanksgiving weekend by going over to Grammie's home and taking her down to their home in Guysborough. Her parents were already there, and the house was warm and cozy when they arrived. The fireplace was lit, and Grammie settled in a comfort-able chair by the warm fire, where she could look out the window and view the beautiful Milford Haven River. She felt that, if God had made a more stunning place, she had yet to see it. Ann brought her a hot cup of tea and a fresh cookie. Grammie was happy.

It was still early in the afternoon, and Ann decided to go for a ride on her bicycle. She donned her walking shoes, a jacket, and a cap, and took off for the river. As she approached it, she saw someone sitting on a rock by the edge of the water.

She was not sure whether she should go there or not, but as she got closer, she realized it was Shane. He jumped up when he saw her, and it was quite evident that he was pleased to see her.

"Well, I didn't expect to see you here!" he exclaimed. "Are you here for the holiday?"

"Yes, I am. My parents and grandmother are here as well. I wouldn't miss coming here for Thanksgiving. It's the true end of summer when we celebrate this holiday. The weather is so beautiful. It's almost like a day in summer. I'm really glad to see you. How have you been? Are you still writing?"

"Woah! one question at a time, please. I'm fine and I am still writing, but I just hit a snag with it and came down here to see if I could find a way to continue on."

"You look tired! You must be working too hard. Take a day or two away from your writing, and you'll find it will clear your mind. A change of scenery is as good as a rest," ventured Ann.

"You're probably right," he said. "Let's go for a ride on our bikes. You lead the way, and I'll follow."

He let Ann go first and rode behind her for a short distance, then he pulled up beside her and they started to talk, discussing what had happened in each of their lives since they had last been together. Ann always felt so much at ease with Shane. They seemed to think alike and were interested in the same things. It was as though she had known him all her life. It was a bit of a strange feeling. She had never felt that way about anyone before. She liked him; she really did. It was as though they had a common bond.

They rode along the river and then turned for home. As they arrived at the juncture in their driveways, they stopped.

"Thank you for finding me on the shore. I needed that break from my writing. You were right. I think it did clear my mind. My parents are here now. I think I'll just forget my writing for a day or two as you suggested, have some supper, watch some television, and get a good night's sleep. Do you have anything special planned for tomorrow?"

"I've had every day planned since school started. It's a bit hard on the nerves, so I left these few days to do as I please. Why? What do you have in mind?"

Shane thought for a few seconds. "I've been thinking. We live almost next door to each other. In fact, we partly share the same driveway. I think it would be nice if we all got together for a meal. It doesn't have to be something fancy, just a friendly get together. What do you think?"

"I think it's a great idea," said Ann. "I'll talk it over with my mother and get back to you. Can we meet again tomorrow?"

Shane looked pleased. "Yes, we can. That would be great. I think my parents would love that. They've often said they'd like to meet their neighbours across the way and this would be their chance," answered a beaming Shane. Then he gave her a hug and hopped back on his bike.

"I'll call you in the morning," he said as he rode off on his bike and disappeared from sight. Ann rode up the driveway, parked her bike by the deck, and entered the house.

Her parents and grandmother were sitting in the living room by the fireplace watching television, and she joined them for a short time. Then she realized she hadn't had supper so she went out to the kitchen to make herself a sandwich. Barbara followed her and filled the teapot with water and put it on the stove to heat.

"Did you enjoy your bike ride?" Barbara asked.

"Yes, I did," she said. "When I got to the river, Shane was there. He was taking a break from his writing and was more than pleased for the company. We talked for a while and then went for a ride around the river. He asked me something, and I'm going to see what you think. He would like for you, Dad, and Grammie to meet his parents. He suggested a meal of some sort, nothing fancy, he said. What do you think?"

"I think it's a great idea," said Barbara. "I've been making the same suggestion to your father. I have an idea of my own. Why don't we invite them to Thanksgiving dinner? I have to cook dinner anyway, and it would be a good time to do that. Do you think that's possible?"

"Oh, Mom, that's a great idea, and I'm sure they would like it."

Ann was very pleased. This was sounding better than she had hoped for. She decided she would go up with Shane when they returned from their bike ride the next day and invite them herself.

"Thanks, Mom. You're the greatest! I'll pitch in and help, and I am sure Grammie will peel vegetables."

Barbara nodded. "I'll make a couple pumpkin pies and some fresh biscuits tomorrow. We have everything else. I brought everything for a good dinner with me. You do the inviting. This could be very nice. I was wondering how we could get to meet them."

Ann went to bed feeling glad Shane had come up with a way for the families to finally meet. That Shane was a smart man!

The next day was Sunday, and before Ann had breakfast, Shane phoned and asked if she would rather go for a drive than a bike ride. She said she would love to do that but first she had to visit his parents.

He said he would pick her up in an hour, to which she responded that she would be ready.

Shane arrived on time, and they made the trip up the hill to see his parents first. Ann had not met them before and immediately came to the conclusion that they were a handsome couple. His father was taller than Shane and very slim. Shane had his deep blue eyes and curly, brown hair, and when they shook hands, she noticed his hands also had the long slim fingers of a musician. Shane's hands were a repeat of his father's. His mother was a very small, slim woman, with a warm smile that made you feel it was a privilege for her to meet you. They were a striking couple.

Ann delivered her message on behalf of her parents and herself, and they graciously accepted. They made small talk for a few minutes, and then Shane and Ann left for their day of adventure.

Ann settled back in the seat and left Shane to do the driving. As usual, there was no shortage of conversation, and as they drove, Shane asked her if there was any special place she would like to go.

"Have you even been to Sherbrooke Village?" she asked.

"No, I haven't. I've always wanted to go there but never had the chance. Would you like to go there?"

"Yes, I would. I've never been there either. I'm like you. I never had the chance."

Shane drove to Guysborough, through the Nine Mile Woods, and the Twelve Mile Woods to Highway 7, and then on to Sherbrooke. They spent several hours at the museum, which is Nova Scotia's largest provincial museum. They visited many of the twenty-five heritage buildings, each with costumed interpreters, and had their picture taken with a 1905-type camera. They ate lunch at the village restaurant and browsed the company store.

It was starting to get later in the day, so they drove further toward the coast and stopped at the Liscombe Lodge and Convention Centre in Liscombe Mills, where they enjoyed a delicious dinner of lobster with all the trimmings. The sun was setting as they left the centre, and they delighted in the sunset over the water as they drove along the coast to Goldboro and on to Larry's River and back to Guysborough. It was a day to remember, not inasmuch as it was something they had never done before but because they had done it together and had enjoyed their day to the fullest.

Shane drove Ann home. They sat in the car for a few minutes and talked about their day. It seemed as though neither wanted to call it a day. Finally, Ann said she had better go as she had a busy day coming up. The held each other close for a few minutes, kissed, and then parted. It would always be a day they would remember and look back on as one of the nicest they had ever spent together. It was obvious they cared very deeply for each other and thoroughly enjoyed their time together.

It was Thanksgiving Day and Ann, Grammie, and Barbara were busy in the kitchen preparing for the dinner. Dinner was to be at noon, as Ann and her parents had to leave that evening for home. Grammie did the peeling of vegetables. Barbara was in charge of the turkey, and Ann set the table and did most of the running.

Everything was either ready or about to be when the Robertsons arrived. The two couples seemed to be at ease with each other immediately, and Shane and Ann were relieved and happy about that. The meal went as planned, and the two couples chatted away the afternoon. They were really in sync, and it was plain to see they would be friends and good neighbours. Shane whispered to Ann that he would meet her at the junction in the driveway in an hour, and she agreed. Then he and his parents left.

Ann helped her mother clean up and then rode her bike down the driveway. Shane was waiting for her. They spent the remainder of the daylight hours on the shore, talking about their afternoon and how much their parents had enjoyed their time together. Then it was getting dark so they rode back up the driveway. Ann had to prepare to leave to be at school the next day, and Shane had to get back to his writing. They both felt it was a great weekend.

TUESDAY MORNING FOUND ANN back at school. It was all work from here to Christmas, with midterm tests and extracurricular activities taking up most of her time. She still had her violin lessons and her work at home to do as well. During this period, she had very little time for relaxation.

The time passed quickly, and before Ann knew it, Christmas was almost here. She finished school on December twentieth, which gave her a few days before she would pick Grammie up and would head for Guysborough, where the family was spending the holidays. She finished her Christmas shopping, tidied up her house, and was off to her grandmother's home. Grammie was ready when she arrived, and she had some big news for her.

A film company was still interested in doing the film on her great-grandfather, and since Ann was the only one in her family who played the violin, they insisted she should do that part for them. Ann was stunned. She had put it completely from her mind, having never in her wildest dreams expected to be asked to do something like that. She had to see the letter for herself. Grammie produced the letter, and Ann sat as she read it.

This was out of the question. She did not feel she was good enough to play for something of this caliber. Did they realize what they were expecting of her? She was an amateur. She had never played in public before in her life. This would require a great deal of thought. At least she had the Christmas vacation to think about it. She would discuss it with her family and get their opinions. It would be an experience, and she would love to do it, but if she did, it would have to be perfection, and she would need a good accompanist. She had no idea who could possibly fit that position.

Ann made sure Grammie had done everything, including locking both her doors and putting the key in the special spot in her purse, before they left for Guysborough. As usual, they stopped in Antigonish for lunch, and then drove on to their home on the hill. The river was frozen over in part but was still pretty as any picture one could imagine. Bill and Barbara were already there and the house was all decorated for

Christmas. Bill loved to be outdoors and the outside of the house was as well decorated as the inside. Ann decided she would have to take a drive across the river to see their house from the other side.

There was a stunning fir Christmas tree in one corner of the living room. Ann distributed Grammie's and her presents under it and then went on into the kitchen to see if there was anything she could do to help her mother. As usual, Grammie had settled into a comfortable chair by the fireplace. She was happy to enjoy the warm fire and the elegantly decorated tree.

Ann found her mother in the kitchen baking Christmas cookies. She situated herself on a stool, and they talked while the cookies were baking. Ann told Barbara about the letter Grammie had received, and the request that was made for her to play her great-grandfather's piece of music during the film. Barbara was so pleased and proud to hear this. She told her mother they would discuss it when Christmas Day was over, but for now, they would just think about it.

Barbara told her they had an invitation for Christmas dinner at the Robertsons' home, so she thought she would invite them over Christmas Eve for a few drinks and probably some holiday food. She told Ann she would leave it to her to do the inviting. Ann agreed to do that. She knew she would be seeing Shane soon, as he knew when she was arriving.

The two families enjoyed Christmas Eve together. They drank, ate, and told stories, and it almost seemed as though they had known one another all their lives. Ann had brought her violin with her and played some Christmas carols for them. Shane was amazed at her ability to play. He knew she played the violin but was certainly not aware of how well she played. He enjoyed her playing but said nothing. Maybe, just maybe, he had a surprise in store for her too.

Shane and his parents left about midnight, with Ann and her family promising to be at their place at four p.m. the next day for dinner. Ann and Barbara cleaned up in the kitchen and then sat by the fireplace, discussing the evening with their newfound friends. They went to bed with the feeling that it was going to be a nice Christmas.

Christmas was a beautiful, crisp, sunny winter day. By nine o'clock in the morning, they were all gathered around the Christmas tree to open gifts. After the gifts were all open and all the oohs and aahs were over, Ann and Barbara left for the kitchen to prepare a nice brunch.

Three o'clock approached, and they left for the Robertsons. Before they left, Ann had a call from Shane asking her if she would bring her violin with her, and of course, she obliged. As they drove up the hill to the Robertsons' home, they were amazed at how beautiful the place looked. They had gone all out in their decorations. Everything was perfection. As they entered the house, they realized not only were the decorations outside stunning but the inside ones were like something one would see in a magazine as well. Ann mentioned to Shane that they would have to make a trip to the other side of the river and view both properties from across the water. He agreed that they would do that as soon as dinner was over.

The Christmas dinner with all the trimmings was an absolute

masterpiece, and the company made it perfection. There never was a Christmas dinner any one of them enjoyed more.

With dinner over, Barbara and Shane's mother, Elsie, left for the kitchen to clean up while Ann and Shane went off to view the lights of their respective homes from the opposite side of the river. They both agreed that their two houses made a noticeably festive sight from afar and were proud of what their parents had accomplished. Soon they were all back in the Robertsons' living room, and all of a sudden, Ann noticed a piano in one corner of the large room.

"Who plays the piano?" she asked.

"Mom does," Shane answered.

"Oh no," Elsie replied. "I do play a little, but Shane is the pianist in the family. He's a great player. Writing and playing the piano are the two loves of his life."

"Well, come on, Shane," Ann said. "Let us hear you play. I played for your family. Now it's your turn to play for mine."

Shane didn't need a second invitation. He sat at the piano and played. He sounded great, just like a concert pianist. He was a natural. He had a gift very few people have. The music just seemed to flow from his fingertips as they touched the keyboard. Shane thought Ann was good. Ann thought he was spectacular. She could listen to him play all evening.

"Wow! You're terrific," said Barbara. "You never told us you played the piano. You didn't even say anything when Ann played for you last evening. Why?"

Shane looked a little sheepish. "After I heard Ann play last evening, I thought, *I will never be able to play as well as she can.* I asked Ann to bring her violin with her today. Perhaps we can play a piece or two together. How about playing with me, Ann?"

"Oh, I'd love to do that," answered Ann, as she went to get her violin. "What should we play?"

"You play whatever you want, and I'll accompany you," replied Shane, as he settled himself on the piano bench. Ann made sure her violin was in tune with the piano and then started to play. They played one piece after another to the absolute pleasure of their families. However, no one enjoyed it more than Shane and Ann.

They were almost finished playing when Ann played the piece of music she had found in the old violin case. Shane looked startled and almost stopped playing. He knew the music and played it himself, but he had never heard it played by anyone else before. *Where did she get that piece of music?* The thought kept racing through his head as he accompanied her. They finished playing and silence fell over the two families.

"Ann, where did you get that piece of music?" Shane asked her.

"I found that music inside the case for this old violin. This violin belonged to my great-grandfather, Alex Blair. He wrote it. I'm surprised that you seemed to know it. Have you ever heard it before?"

He shook his head. "I've never heard anyone play it before. I have many music books for the piano, but I have never come across it in any book. I found that piece of music, written by hand, in an old book owned, at one time, by my great-grandmother Mary Morgan. She was a violinist and played for a number of years, and then all of a sudden, she disappeared from the music world. I really don't know much about her, other than that she had a daughter named Susan Morgan, my grandmother. I've never heard anyone mention who her father was, and I guess I never thought much about it. I wonder why my great-grandmother and your great-grandfather both happen to have that piece of music."

They both knew it was a beautiful and special piece, and they played it over several more times. The evening that had started out as a wonderful time between friends ended in the same way, but it seemed to be completed with a bit of mystery attached. However, it was put aside for the time being as the Blair family left for home, thanking the Robertsons for the delicious dinner and a wonderful Christmas Day.

As the parents exchanged goodbyes, Shawn whispered to Ann that he would see her the next day.

They drove home with the feeling they had a Christmas day that would be difficult to forget. Ann helped her grandmother get ready for bed as it had been a long day for her, but it was quite evident that she had thoroughly enjoyed it. After tucking Grammie in for the night, she went to get ready for bed herself. She was soon in bed and sound asleep.

The day after Christmas was what the Robertson family often referred to as a "lazy day." They were still full of turkey and the trimmings from the previous day, and so it was a day for some extra sleep or a good walk. Ann and Shane decided on the walk in the fresh air and the chance to be together.

A walk to the shoreline was a little too cold for this time of year, so they drove to the village of Guysborough and walked around the village, taking in the Christmas decorations. They had their skates with them, so they donned them and went for a skate on the outside rink near the high school. Before going home, they stopped at the restaurant there and enjoyed a piece of hot mincemeat pie with whipped cream and a cup of coffee.

They drove back to Ann's home, and talked for a few minutes longer before Shane pulled her into his arms and kissed her. They held each other for another minute or two, and then Ann went up to her house. She turned and waved to him as he drove away.

DURING LUNCH ON ONE of Ann's last days before heading back home, the subject of her taking part in the movie on her great-grandfather was discussed. After hearing everyone's opinion, Ann made up her mind that she would try to do what the film producers had requested of her. She had given it quite a lot of thought on her own and talked it over with Shane. He agreed that it was a chance of a lifetime, and she should go for it.

Finally, Ann decided she would go and represent the family. It would be a challenge, but as Shane said, it was the "chance of a lifetime." There were a number of arrangements she would have to make, and many hours of work to prepare for leaving her students for a period of time with a substitute teacher, but she felt she could handle it.

Rather than have Grammie write them and then wait for the studio to get back to her, Ann composed a message on her computer and sent it on Grammie's behalf. She asked for the length of time she would be expected to be there and all the particulars regarding her stay. Since she had to ask for the time off from her teaching position, she had to know these things before she brought it to her principal. She went to bed that evening a little nervous about the whole thing but also a little excited. She was going to be in a movie. It was a small part, but an important one.

The next day, she called Shane to tell him she had decided to take the part. He told her he just knew she was making the right decision and was sure she would do fine.

"Thanks, Shane," she said. "I feel better about my decision now. I guess I needed your vote of confidence."

"I will be over later to talk with you," Shane said. "I have some news too. I'll be there in a little while."

As promised, Shane arrived at the Blair residence around seven and invited Ann to go for a drive with him. Without any hesitation, she donned her coat, boots, and gloves, and the two of them left.

Shane drove to the end of the driveway and stopped the car.

Ann looked at him. "I don't know whether to be happy or worried. What's your big news?"

"Well, as you know, I just sent my last novel to the printers, and

I'm ready to start my next one, which takes place in Africa. The day after tomorrow, I'm flying out there. I need to visit the place where my story is taking place to get the feel of it, and the best way to do that is to visit the place and see for myself. I will probably be gone for about two months."

This was a big surprise to Ann. In fact, she was shocked. She had no idea he would be leaving for that length of time. She would really miss his company. It finally really dawned on her how she was beginning to feel about him. He was beginning to be a very important part of her life.

Ann looked shocked and was almost at a loss for words. "Two months! I … wasn't expecting that. I will miss you … very much." She looked as though she was about to cry.

Shane was surprised and looked at her for a few seconds. "Ann, I had no idea you would feel this way. Right now, I can't decide whether I'm feeling sorry for you or happy for me. I know how I feel about you, but had no idea if you felt the same."

He wrapped his arms around her, and they just sat there for a few minutes, not saying anything but enjoying the closeness.

Finally, Ann moved and managed to say, "Shane, I care very much for you, and I will miss you, but I know travelling to different places is part of your writing, and I understand. Just be careful and be safe. Keep in touch with home, and I will look forward to your return."

Less than two days later, Shane was on his way to Africa.

THE FIRST OF JANUARY, Ann was back at her job and dealing with all the things associated with the middle of any school year. She was still busy with her violin lessons and the normal everyday happenings associated with life in general. She heard from Shane whenever he had the chance to get in contact with her. She lived for his calls, and with every call, she missed him more.

It was nearly two months before Grammie heard back from the movie company. Barbara called Ann to tell her that her grandmother had the letter with the necessary information enclosed. Ann told her mother she would be down to Guysborough on Saturday, weather permitting.

Saturday arrived, the weather was fine, and Ann was off to Guysborough. She loved spending time in her new home there, and it did not take her long to decide to visit it. Her parents and Grammie had been there since Christmas. They seemed to like it better there than their own homes. She spent a pleasant Saturday evening with them and the Robertsons and left on Sunday after lunch to go back to her house, armed with the information Grammie had received from the movie company.

Upon arriving home, the first thing she did was sit down and study the information from the Memory Lane Movie Company, which was situated in New York. She was to arrive by the first of April and would be there about six weeks. She would have an accompanist of their choosing. Her accommodations were already booked. She would be staying near the studio, with transportation provided. Her plane ticket would arrive shortly.

The next day of school, she visited the principal's office, told him all her information, and asked for the time away from her job. He was very pleased for her and said he would get back to her as quickly as possible, probably within the next day or two, as he would have to take it to the school board. She told him she would have everything ready for her substitute teacher, so things could carry on as usual.

She left his office with a good feeling about the situation.

The Trip

THE DAY FINALLY ARRIVED, and Ann was off to New York. She had not travelled alone very much and had butterflies in her stomach. She wondered if she had packed everything she would need. She tried to be sure everything in her house was taken care of—all lights off, furnace turned to the proper temperature, and everything that would spoil removed from the refrigerator.

Her mind was racing at top speed, but she left feeling secure that she had tended to everything. She checked her purse to make sure she had her passport, plane ticket, bank card, and some cash. She placed her suitcase, small carry on, and violin in the car. Then she threw the strap of her purse over her shoulder and jumped into her father's car, as he was driving her to the airport. She heaved a sigh of relief as she settled into her seat. Now she could relax for a little while.

As she was flying United, she landed at JFK International Airport and took a taxi from there to the Sheraton Lincoln Harbor Hotel about twenty-five kilometres from the airport. Ann had never been to New York alone before and was amazed at the changes since she had last visited. The taxi driver assisted her into the hotel lobby, and she was on her own from there.

She checked in and was escorted to her room. The accommodations provided for her were all anyone could ask for. She was given a spacious bedroom with a large closet. The bathroom was equipped with all the things she could possibly need, and off the bedroom was a sitting room with a very large television and the type of furniture anyone would love to have in their own home. Ann was completely surprised and satisfied and was beginning to feel completely comfortable and at ease in her new, away-from-home abode. She immediately felt she was going to be well cared for here.

The first thing she did was to empty her suitcases, hang her clothes in the closet, and arrange her other things in the drawers of the huge dresser. She put her personal things in the bathroom, and just as she finished, the phone rang.

It was a Mr. Melvin Wright, one of the producers of the movie. He asked if he could take her to lunch so they could talk. He wanted her to get to know some of the people associated with the movie and to make an appointment for her to meet the man who would be accompanying her as she played the violin.

"I will be there in ten minutes," answered Ann. "How will I know you?"

"Don't worry. I know most of the people here, or at least have seen them before. I will find you."

"I'll be there," answered Ann and hung up the phone.

Ten minutes later found Ann standing in the lobby of the hotel. People were milling around. Everyone seemed to know where they were going. It was a big place, and Ann realized it would take some getting used to. She noticed a well-dressed, middle-aged man standing off to one side of the lobby surveying the people as they passed through. At the same time, he noticed Ann. He walked toward her, and she realized he must be the person she was looking for. He was very pleasant-looking, and as he approached her, he smiled.

"Are you Ann Blair?"

"Yes, I am."

He extended his hand and introduced himself.

"Hello, I'm Melvin Wright, one of the producers of the show. It is so nice to meet you."

"Hello. It's nice to meet you too."

Mr. Wright ushered Ann into the hotel restaurant for lunch and a place to talk.

Melvin Wright had greyish brown hair and a mustache. He was casually dressed in tan pants with a dark brown sports jacket and a pale green shirt with no tie. He was a very pleasant-looking gentleman, which made Ann feel somewhat at ease. He asked the waitress to seat them in a reasonably quiet spot where they could talk. She handed them the lunch menu and left them to decide what they would like

"Have you been to New York before?" Mr. Wright asked Ann.

"Yes, I have, but it was a few years ago. I was quite young then, probably just barely a teenager. I really don't remember if it was this part of New York."

Ann was starting to feel more at ease with him. He was the type of person who could make one feel comfortable. He seemed like an uncle you had not seen for some time and who was anxious to please you.

The waitress came back, and they ordered lunch. Ann was not really hungry so she ordered a salad and coffee. Mr. Wright said he had not eaten all day so he ordered a hearty lunch with tea.

That being done, Mr. Wright settled back in his chair. "Now, Ann," he said, "tell me all about this piece of music you found that was written by your great-grandfather."

Ann was glad he had asked her something she would have no trouble with. That was something she knew well and had no problem in relating the story to her companion. He listened intently as she relayed her account of how she came into possession of the piece of music that was written by her great-grandfather.

He told her it was the only part of the story her grandmother's account was rather vague on. He needed the true story here to be able to finish the movie.

They talked for some time. Mr. Wright asked many questions, and Ann was able to supply the answers. He made some notes on what she had related to him and then accompanied Ann back to her hotel room, informing her that he would come for her in the morning, around nine o'clock, and accompany her to the location where the movie was being filmed.

Ann spent the remainder of the day in her room. She watched some television and then went down to the dining room for some dinner. She was not one who liked to eat alone, especially in a strange place, but in this case, she had no choice. She finished her meal and retired to her room.

There was a large inviting bathtub in her bathroom. She filled it with really warm water, splashed in some nice-smelling bubble bath, and crawled into the luxurious perfumed water. It was so relaxing. Ann soaked for some time before she pulled the plug to let the water out, dried herself on one of the huge towels provided, and slipped into her nightgown and housecoat. Then she brushed her hair, brushed her teeth, turned the bedclothes down, climbed into bed, and turned the television on. She watched a program and found she was getting sleepy, so she turned the television off and was soon fast asleep.

Ann was up early the next morning. She was washed and dressed by seven thirty. She picked up her wallet and key and went down to breakfast. At nine o'clock, she was standing in the lobby waiting for Mr. Wright, who was right on time. He hailed a taxi, and they were driven to the studio where the movie was being filmed.

This was the first time Ann had ever been in such a place, and she felt a little uneasy. If she were placed in a classroom with a group of grade-nine youths, she would feel right at home, but this was out of her league. She felt very much the outsider. This was going to take a lot of getting used to. Perhaps she had "bitten off more than she could chew" as the saying goes. Then she thought of Grammie and what she would tell her. Grammie would tell her to "grab the bull by the horns and get in there and do the job."

I will do that, thought Ann.

Mr. Wright introduced her to some of the actors taking parts in the film and then went to look for the one who would be accompanying her on piano. Ann could not help but wishing it was Shane who would be playing with her, but Shane was a writer first, and he had that to take care of.

Everyone seemed to know what they were to do except Ann. She stood off to one side and watched as the others rushed here and there. They stopped to speak to one another for a minute or two and then continued on their way. All of a sudden, Melvin Wright appeared. He had a man with him. Ann thought he was just about the most handsome man she had ever seen.

Melvin introduced them. "Ann, this is Colin Watson. He will be accompanying you on the piano. Colin, this is Ann Blair. She is playing the piece of music we talked about, on the violin. You are to be her accompanist. She will show you the music."

Ann put out her hand to shake hands with him and looked into the most piercing blue eyes she had ever seen. His eyes seemed almost to be smiling. He had dark, wavy, short hair and a beautiful smile with even white teeth. He stood over six feet tall and had a lean body with the muscles of an athlete. He exuded confidence and seemed in every way to be the perfect gentleman. Ann thought that, if there were such a thing as the perfect man, he was that person.

Melvin left Ann and Colin to get acquainted and went to attend to some other business.

"Would you like a cup of coffee?" Colin asked Ann.

"That would be nice," she answered.

They walked across the street to a little café and sat in a spot where they could talk and get to know one another. As they would be working together for the next few weeks, it only made sense that they should know a little about the person they were working with. Colin ordered coffee for each of them, and they settled down for some easy talk. Ann found she was getting more at ease with him and finding that he was really quite friendly.

She found out a little about his personal life. He was married and had two children, a son and a daughter. He lived in California and had been an actor since he was a teenager. He loved what he did for a living, but it took him away from his family for long periods of time, and he sometimes felt that was not good with two young children at home. It left a big responsibility to his wife of twelve years.

Colin found out that Ann was from Nova Scotia and was a high-school mathematics teacher. She was not married and was a great-granddaughter of Alex Blair, the man the film was about. He found out something else that was very interesting to him: Ann owned and played his violin. He was very anxious to see it. She told him it was at the hotel and he would certainly get to see it and even play it if he wanted to.

He played the piano and guitar. Those were the two instruments he was interested in and fairly good at, but he could play a few tunes on the violin as well. They spent a couple of hours getting to know one another. In that period of time, they found out that they were quite amicable and liked each other. Working together would be an experience for both of them, and since they were from two different worlds, they could probably learn a great deal from each other.

The afternoon was spent sitting in on meetings. Ann was given her script. It was not a large speaking part, as her main role was to play the piece of music on the old violin. Colin's role was mostly opposite Ann's, which made it easy for them to work together. Colin felt his main concern was to learn to accompany Ann as she played, and since he had not yet seen what he was to play, it worried him a little. However, they would get to that when the time came.

Upon leaving the meeting, Ann went back to her hotel room to freshen up before dinner. Then she went down to the hotel dining room, expecting to eat alone. Then Colin walked in. He noticed Ann, and that she had no one with her. He made his way to her table and asked if there was anyone dining with her. She told him she was eating alone.

"So am I. Do you mind if I join you?"

"Of course not, please sit down. I would love some company," she said.

He pulled out a chair and sat with her. Now that they had spent some time together, Ann found it much easier to talk with him. They ordered dinner and chatted away throughout their meal. On first meeting Colin, Ann had thought he was a bit intimidating, but the more she got to know him, the more she felt he was a very nice person.

She was beginning to think he would be pleasant and quite helpful to work with. As they ate and talked away, she was starting to look forward to their time together. She understood that he was a very accomplished pianist. This would probably be a chance for her to learn more as she played her violin with his accompaniment.

They spent a couple hours at the meal. He told her about his wife, daughter, and son. They were his life, and even though he loved acting, his greatest joy was returning home to his family. His wife was a stay-at-home mom. She was a great seamstress and sometimes did a bit of sewing for friends and neighbours, but it was not a full-time job. She just did it because she liked that type of work. She was active in their church and the PTA. This took up a great deal of her time. She was a terrific mother and her children always came first.

His son, Conor, who was twelve, and daughter, Emma, who was ten, did not require the attention they had needed when they were younger, and this gave his wife, Eleanor, more time to herself. Ann listened with intent as he talked about his family. She could see he was very proud of them and loved them very much.

As Colin finished telling her about his family, Colin asked Ann to tell him something about her life. She told him she was from Pictou

County in Nova Scotia and her parents were Bill and Barbara Blair. Her father was retired, and they lived close to where she taught, but she had her own place close to the school.

She told him about visiting her grandmother and finding the violin played by her great-grandfather Alex Blair. Colin was especially enthralled when she mentioned about finding the papers in the old violin case. He asked many questions as she told the story of her great-grandfather having the cottage on the hill overlooking the Guysborough River, and how she and her parents had made it into a lovely home. She also mentioned Shane Robertson and the gorgeous home he and his parents had next to theirs, and that, in fact, they shared part of the same driveway.

"Shane Robertson… Where have I heard that name before?" asked Colin.

"He's a writer and has written a number of novels. In fact, he's in Africa right now working on his next one. He just finished one when we were in Guysborough during Christmas. He is also an excellent pianist. He happened to have the same piece of music I found in the violin case. We are still wondering how this happened. It's a mystery we're working on."

It was getting late and the waitresses were starting to clear their table, asking them if they wanted anything else. They figured it was a hint for them to leave. They left the restaurant, and Ann started for her room. At first it seemed he was following her, almost to her door, but then she realized his room was next door to hers. All the people working in the movie were on the same floor.

"Goodnight, Ann. I will see you in the morning, and we'll get to work on that piece of music. I'm looking forward to hearing it."

"Goodnight," Ann answered. "I hope I can play it as well as I should for you. Time will tell, and I will see you in the morning."

Ann closed her door and made sure it was locked. She now seemed to be less worried about playing for Colin, even though she felt he would be a perfectionist. She prepared for bed and watched television for an hour or so, and then turned off the light and fell asleep.

THE NEXT MORNING, ANN was up early and ready for breakfast by seven thirty. She walked down to the restaurant and sat at a table by the window. It was a bright sunny morning with a slight breeze. A small bird Ann did not recognize sat on the window sill near her table. It seemed to be giving her the same puzzled look she was giving it. Then it shook its head and flew off. The waitress came at that point. She ordered orange juice, toast, and coffee. Just as her order arrived, Colin appeared on the scene.

"Do you mind if I sit with you?" he asked

"No, not at all," responded Ann.

The waitress returned. He ordered and then they started talking over their plans for the day.

"There is a room with a piano we can use, close to where we're filming. It's not far. We can walk if you wish."

"That will be fine," said Ann. "I will need to go back to my room to brush my teeth and get my violin. I'll do that while you finish eating." She left for her room and within a few minutes was back.

They walked to their destination and talked all the way. They had no problem finding things to talk about, and before they knew it, they were there.

The room was small, but in the centre was a grand piano, which took up much of the room. Ann took her violin out of the case, and Colin was right there to see it.

"Wow!" he said. "It's a nice-looking violin. If it could talk, just think of the miles it has travelled and the stories it could tell. Do you mind if I look at it?"

Ann handed him the violin.

"Go ahead and try it," she said, placing the bow in his hand.

"First of all, let's make sure it's in tune."

He gave the violin back to Ann while he sat at the piano, and she made sure they were in tune with each other. It needed very little change. She handed the violin back to Colin. He took it and began to play. He played a familiar tune and sounded quite good. It was obvious he was very musical, and though the piano might be his instrument, it would take very little to make him quite good on the violin as well.

"You are good on the violin. Perhaps we can play a duet before we're finished."

"The piano has always been my first love, but I like the violin as well. Maybe one day I'll pay more attention to it. My daughter, Emma, is very good on the piano, and my son, Conor, likes the violin. He's very good as well. However, they are both into sports and time for music is at a minimum. I try to keep encouraging them, but I don't want to push too hard. Okay, that is enough about my life. Where is that piece of music? Let's get to work."

Ann produced the music, and he studied it for a few minutes.

"It's my job to accompany, so I will have to figure that out for myself. You'll have to play it for me. I have to warn you though, you may be tired of it before we get it the way we want it to sound."

Ann played the piece for him. He listened intently. She played it over several times, and each time, she could almost see him memorizing the music. She was sure he had a great ear and took in every note. She stopped and put the violin down.

"You are very good," he said. "You did a terrific job of playing that piece of music. Your great-grandfather would be very proud if he were here to listen to you play it. I just hope I can do it justice. I'm going to ask you to play it several times again, and I'll record it. That way I can figure out how I want to accompany you."

He turned on his recorder, and Ann played the piece again several times.

"That's fine," he said. "Now I can work on it and won't need to have you sit here and be bored to death."

"Oh, don't worry about that," said Ann. "I love to listen to you play. I'm sure it won't take you long before you have it perfect."

They worked on their lines for some time and then parted, Ann off to read and study her lines and Colin to work on the accompaniment for the music.

Ann had lunch and returned to her room. She knew Colin was a perfectionist and knew she was the same, although possibly not as severe as Colin.

She thought it was probably the teacher in her. She always figured that, if you got something the best it could possibly be, then you must have it right. She had a feeling Colin would carry the perfection to the limit.

They spent several days working together. Each day they got to know one another better. Ann was beginning to really like him. He was a good listener. He asked questions but was never prying. He showed an interest in her violin playing. He asked if she had someone to accompany her when she was home. She told him about Shane and what a great pianist he was. He wanted to know if Shane was someone special.

"He is a very special friend. We spend a great amount of time together when we're at our homes in Guysborough, and we're very fond of each other. As I already told you, Shane is a writer and travels a great deal when he's not writing. He likes to visit the areas he uses as a setting for his novels and get the feel of the place for himself. According to his mother, writing and playing the piano are his two loves."

They worked hard on their music, and soon it was as well played as anyone could do. Colin recorded their playing and listened to it many times over. There were a few times when he asked Ann to play with him again while he recorded. Finally, it was to his satisfaction. He liked what he heard, and when that happened, he'd learned from the past that it should be left alone. He firmly believed in the saying, "If it ain't broke, don't fix it!"

Time was winding down. Colin had a few short parts throughout the film but his main part was with Ann near the end. Ann was to appear as Colin's very special friend. That was made apparent, especially toward the end, but their main part was to play the special piece of music written by Alex Blair. They played their best, and every eye and ear on the set was transfixed on them as they clearly played as well as any musician could. They played as one, each in complete connection with the other. It was phenomenal.

The film ended with the two of them sharing a kiss. They did so, as was required, but it was quite evident that their shared kiss meant more to each of them than the film required. It completely shocked Colin, and he left the set in a hurry.

Ann placed her violin back in the case and left through a side door. She hailed a cab and went back to the hotel. She went up to her room, placed her violin on the bed, and left, wandering down to a little brook that ran close to the hotel and sat on a bench. It was quiet and peaceful and gave her time to think about what had just happened.

She really didn't think he could make her feel that way. It was a feeling she'd never had before in her life. He definitely meant more to her than she had anticipated. She knew she liked him, but now she knew it was much more than like. She was in love with him. He was a handsome man, one of the best-looking men she had ever seen. He was kind, thoughtful, generous, knowledgeable, friendly, and loving. He was a true gentleman.

But he was a married man. He loved his wife and children. They were his whole life - his joy. He lived to get back home to them. He loved them dearly, and nothing on earth would ever keep him away from them. To picture him as being any other type of person would be taking away from him the very essence of who he was. There were very few people in this world with the principles he had, and he lived by them.

COLIN PULLED HIMSELF TOGETHER and returned to the set. Most of the cast had gone. He asked one of the remaining ones if they had seen Ann and was told she was seen leaving in a cab about an hour earlier. He figured she was back at the hotel, so he took a cab back to the hotel and went up to his room. After sitting on the bed for a short time, he decided he just had to go talk to her. Reluctantly, he knocked on her door.

He didn't favour going into her room and planned to ask her to go for a walk with him. After knocking several times and getting no answer, he wandered outside and decided to walk down to the brook and sit on one of the benches for a little while. As he got nearer to the brook and the benches, he saw Ann sitting by herself just gazing into space. He sat down beside her.

After a few minutes, he quietly said, "What happened back there …

that was something I didn't foresee, not from you and not from myself. There's something more here than we expected."

"I know," Ann said quietly. "It took me by complete surprise. I'm sorry!"

"Don't be sorry. It wasn't your fault. It was mine. When I got into films and there were times when I had to kiss the actress working opposite me, I made three promises: First, I promised I would always be true to myself. This is just a job, and I swore I would never become involved with any actress I was working with.

"Next, I made a promise that I would always be true to my wife and children. I would never, ever, do anything to hurt them. They are ... my life. And last, I made a promise that I would never hurt the actress I was working with. I could never hurt anyone in that way. Up until now, I have been successful in keeping those three promises.

"Today, I may have broken all of them. And believe me, it hurts. I hate myself for doing that. Please, don't feel you're to blame. I am the one who's in the wrong. I'm a married man!"

"Please, stop! You're not totally to blame. I'm wrong as well. The truth is that I do care very deeply for you. You're one of the nicest people I have ever met in my life. You're handsome and have all the qualities of a terrific person. I hope your wife appreciates the husband she has." Sighing, Ann finished her little speech and said no more.

They sat in silence for a few minutes. Then Colin asked Ann if she would like to go to dinner, as they had done platonically so many times before. They hadn't eaten since breakfast, and right at that time, a meal seemed like the perfect thing to bring them both back to the way things were before the final take of the film. Ann said that she would like that, but she would prefer to go back to her room to freshen up first. Colin agreed and they walked back to the hotel, agreeing to both be ready in an hour.

An hour later, Colin knocked on her door and she appeared immediately, looking fresh and recovered from their little unexpected incident. He looked as though he had done some freshening up as well and looked less troubled than he had a few hours earlier.

There was no doubt they would discuss what had happened and how they would cope with it, but right now, they were both hungry and looking forward to a nice meal. When they entered the restaurant, there were some other cast members present. They were asked to join them and they did. Colin figured that, if they were with other cast members, it would not appear as though they were having a cozy little dinner by themselves. There was no reason to cause gossip when there was nothing actually happening. He was sure he could handle the situation. The only thing he didn't realize was that he had no experience in this type of role. Never before had he had any feelings for one of the women he was acting with.

This was entirely different. Ann was special. She was a beautiful woman, and in no way had she set out to entice him. It had just happened to her, as it had to him. They were victims of circumstance, and he was sure they were adult enough to deal with the situation.

They chatted with the others and enjoyed their meal. Some of the cast had flights out in the morning. Ann and Colin would be there for two more days. They spent about two hours with their friends and said goodbye to the ones leaving in a few short hours. The remainder were leaving at various times the next day, which would leave them alone for more than a day.

They walked back to their rooms and said goodnight at the door, agreeing to meet for breakfast the next morning. Ann said that she would like to sleep in for an hour or two in the morning, as she was very tired. Colin was too, so they agreed to meet for breakfast at nine o'clock.

Ann closed her door and stood there for a minute or two. She was starting to realize exactly how much she liked Colin's company. He was the kind of person a girl dreams about. The only thing wrong with this was that he was a married man and belonged to someone else. He had made it quite clear that his wife was the love of his life.

The story of my life, thought Ann. She brushed her teeth, donned her nightgown, and crawled into bed. It had been a long and trying day, and she was asleep within minutes.

It was exactly nine o'clock the next morning when he knocked on her door. She was ready and the two of them went off to breakfast. They decided to try some place new this time. Colin had rented a car for two days, and they had driven a few miles before seeing a small restaurant close to the road.

"Oh, that place looks nice," said Ann. "Let's eat there."

Colin agreed and they spent more than an hour relishing a nice breakfast and some time to talk. They always had lots of things to talk about. They were interested in the same things for the most part. He liked to talk about his family, his acting, and his music. She was always interested in hearing him talk about these topics. He in turn liked to hear about her teaching and the many trials and joys involved with it.

He especially loved hearing how she'd found the violin she played and the stories that made up the movie they had just finished about her great-grandfather. She told him about the fact that there were a few mysteries still not solved there. The one that intrigued him most was how she and her neighbour, Shane, happened to have the same piece of music. There had to be a story there, but as yet, no one in the family had found the answer.

By this time, the restaurant was getting quite crowded so they felt they had better move on and take their conversation somewhere else.

They had made no plans for the day. They just wanted to spend the time they had left together. They drove for some time just enjoying the scenery. It took some time before they got out of the city and happened upon a beautiful little park. Colin parked the car and they walked down a narrow path that led to some benches situated beside a wide brook. There were some ducks on the water, and nearby, there was a small shop where one could get food and a few other items. They sauntered into the shop in search of some food to feed the ducks. Fortunately, the shop carried it—probably because it was something most of the visitors there asked for.

Ann purchased the duck food, and they sat on one of the park benches. The ducks were fairly tame and came almost to their feet in search of the food they provided. They seemed to be looking for visitors to bring them a treat, and they twisted their heads and looked at Ann and Colin as their way of saying thank you.

It was a nice little park, well kept with lawns mowed to perfection and flowers and shrubs situated in advantageous spots. Ann and Colin sat there for some time just feeding the ducks and talking. Colin was extremely interested in the fact that Ann's friend Shane and Ann both had copies of that special piece of music. She said that, as far as she knew, the families had never met or known about one another until they met in Guysborough.

She knew how her family happened to be where they were, but she had no idea how the Robertsons happened to build a home there. Shane liked it, because it was a quiet place for him to write, but there were any number of places he could have chosen for that purpose. Why he had chosen that spot was more than she knew. She made up her mind to find the answer to that mystery.

They sat on the bench and fed the ducks for about an hour and then drove on. They had no particular destination in mind. They just wanted to spend the time they had left together, for once they parted, in a little over a day, they believed their paths would never cross again. Ann almost broke into tears every time she thought about it. He was one of the nicest people she had ever met, but he could never be hers.

They drove in silence for a short period of time, and then all of a sudden, Colin pulled to the side of the road and stopped the car.

"Ann," he said, "I would like to go back to that room we practiced in before we played in the movie, and just play. I would like to tape some of our playing and take it home with me."

Ann agreed. She would love to have a tape of some of their music. It would be something she would always have as a keepsake of their time together. They drove back to the hotel, where Ann picked up her violin, and as she left her room, Colin arrived at her door with a guitar in hand.

"Oh," she said, "you brought your guitar with you too."

"Yes, I play the guitar and sing. Perhaps I'll sing some as well. We'll see!" He almost whispered this, as though he didn't want anyone to hear him. They drove on to the studio and got permission to use the room they had used when they were practicing for the movie.

They spent the afternoon and on into the evening playing, with Colin on the piano and Ann with her violin. They played their favourite first, the one composed by Alex Blair. Then they played some classical pieces, some waltzes, some dance music, and also some of the old-time Scottish music, quite common in Nova Scotia.

"That's enough," said Ann. "I want to hear you play your guitar and sing. Come on. Show me how good you are. We'll record that as well."

Colin didn't need much coaxing. He made sure his guitar was in tune, played a few chords, and began to play and sing. Ann was amazed. As good as he was on the piano, she had never even thought of him as a singer as well. He sang a number of songs, and the longer he sang, the better he seemed to sound. It was quite evident that he loved to sing and did a great deal of it. He was a multitalented individual. After a while, he set his guitar down and stood up, which was a clear indication he was finished.

The time passed so quickly they could not believe it when they noticed the sun was setting. Ann said that she was getting hungry, so they picked up the tape and headed off to find a restaurant.

Restaurants were not difficult to find in New York, and soon they were seated at a table in one not too far from their hotel. They ate and discussed the tape they had just made. Colin said he would take it to the nearest music store and have them run off a copy for Ann first thing in the morning. They finished dinner and headed back to the hotel.

Ann knew tomorrow would be their last day together, and that she would have to do her best to put on a brave face. She dreaded having to say goodbye to him. He said goodnight to her at her room door, turned quickly, and disappeared into his own room, shutting the door.

He leaned against it for a few minutes. He was spending time with one of the nicest people he had ever met and enjoying every moment he was with her. The guilt he was feeling was strong. He stood there for a few minutes, deep in thought.

"Why am I feeling guilty?" he said out loud. "I haven't done anything wrong. We haven't done anything wrong. We're just good friends."

THE NEXT MORNING, BOTH Colin and Ann were up early, eager to spend as much time as possible with one another on the last day they would likely ever be together. They met outside their rooms and made their way to the nearest little restaurant for a light breakfast. Colin promised Ann to make her a tape of the music they had played the day before, so that was the first thing to take care of. They found the nearest music store, and it was completed in a very short period of time. Colin handed her the tape, and she slipped it into her pocket. It was one treasure she would always hold on to.

They spent the remainder of the day walking in parks and visiting some of the famous stores in New York City. Ann bought a packaged lunch, and they found a little park tucked away from the bustle of city life. They sat on a bench under a huge tree. They talked nonstop, having so much to say to each other and so little time to say it.

The day passed all too quickly, and before they knew it, their time was running out. Their planes would leave early the next morning, Ann's headed east, and Colin's west. In a few hours, they would be miles apart, each in their own little world. They parted as before at the door to her room. Ann closed her door and started to cry. How would she ever face tomorrow morning? She packed her belongings and went to bed.

THE MORNING ARRIVED AND both she and Colin had to be at the airport by six a.m. Colin was outside her door as she opened it and rolled her suitcase out into the hall. They walked down the hall, took the elevator together, and loaded their belongings into the car. There was not much conversation as they drove to the airport. Each seemed lost in their own little worlds. They checked their luggage and got their boarding passes. Ann had very little time to wait before she boarded her plane, while Colin had about two hours before he boarded his.

They sat off by themselves waiting for Ann to get the call to board. It was as though they had talked themselves out and said very little. Ann was afraid to say much. She was about to cry. Colin held his composure, but as time passed, it was getting more difficult. It was not long before Ann got the call to leave. This was the moment she dreaded.

She stood up. Colin put his arms around her and kissed her on the cheek. She did the same to him. There was no mention of keeping in contact. They both knew their friendship and time together had ended. Ann picked up her overnight bag and her violin, turned, and walked to her boarding gate. She never looked back.

Colin stood there and watched as she went down the ramp. Then he walked to a window and watched her plane until it disappeared from sight. He turned, wiped away a tear that was streaming down his cheek, and walked to his boarding gate. He had never felt that way before in his life. She was someone very special. He knew this was a time in his life he would have to forget. He had a wife and family he loved dearly. But he would tuck Ann away in a special part of his heart, and there she would remain … hurting no one but himself.

Chapter 14

Back Home

ANN ARRIVED HOME, TIRED and a little down, not because she had not accomplished what was expected of her but because she had left behind someone she felt she would never see again. She was certain their paths would never cross in the future and decided what had happened was just one of those things, and she would have to get over it. If it took some time, then so be it.

It was a Saturday, and Ann spent most of the day doing laundry and preparing for her first day back at school. She phoned her substitute and found out where she was to start on Monday morning. That done, she prepared her lesson plans for the start of the week. Her mother phoned to hear all about her trip, and she was on the phone for some time talking with her. After she hung up the phone, she prepared a light supper, had a hot bath, and went to bed. She was very tired, and within minutes sleep overtook her.

Monday morning found her back at school. Her students were glad she was back, and things settled back into routine. It was now only a few weeks before final exams, and the race was on to finish courses for the term. It was a busy time and passed quickly. She made out her final exams, administered them, marked them, and handed in her final marks.

Next, she helped with all the graduation activities, and when the year ended, she was totally exhausted. She took a few days to tidy things up in her house then packed a few things and headed for her home in Guysborough. She loved it there, and it was the perfect place to renew herself.

On her first morning there, she sprang out of bed, washed, brushed her teeth, dressed, and headed down the hill to the river on her bike. As she approached the river, she saw Shane sitting there on a big rock, moving his feet back and forth in the sand.

As soon as she was off her bike, he jumped up and gave her a hug. He was delighted to see her. It was obvious he had missed her. They sat on the sand, and as usual, started to talk. She told him all about her trip, leaving out the parts involving Colin. She was not ready to talk about that yet. It hurt too much.

However, if she told anyone about it, she knew Shane would be the one. She felt he would understand better than anyone. Why? She didn't know. She just felt he was a very compassionate person and would be able to feel what she was feeling.

The time slipped by quickly, and soon they had been on the beach talking for over two hours.

"Did you have breakfast?" Shane asked her.

"No, I didn't. I just wanted to go for a ride to the beach, so I left."

"Let's ride down to that little restaurant and have some breakfast."

"I don't have any money with me."

"I have my wallet. It'll be my treat," Shane said with a big smile.

They rode off down the road, and within a few minutes, reached the restaurant. They entered, found a table close to a window, and ordered breakfast.

Shane noticed that Ann didn't seem to be in as good cheer as she usually was. He asked her if there was anything wrong.

"Why do you ask that?" she questioned.

"You seem a little preoccupied," he answered. "Did something happen when you were in New York? You told me quite a bit about your trip, but I have the feeling you didn't tell the whole story. I know you fairly well. You're quieter than usual. It's not like you to be unhappy. Do you want to talk about it? I'm a good listener, and anything you say to me will never go any further. Trust me."

Ann placed her elbows on the table and rested her head in her hands. She felt it would be good to confide in someone, and she was sure Shane was the right one to bare her soul to. She really trusted him.

"Let's have breakfast first, and then we can go to that little park down the road and talk." She nodded thoughtfully. "I would like to talk to someone."

They ate breakfast and left for the park. As they entered it, Shane notice a bench under a big spruce tree, and they sat there. He let her take the lead. He knew she would tell her story in her own time and in her own way.

When Ann looked at Shane, he could see there were tears just ready to burst forth. He put an arm around her.

"Take your time. We're not in a hurry to go back home."

Ann felt a kind of kinship to Shane. She had not known him for very long but had the feeling she had known him all her life. He had so many traits similar to her father, and hence similar to her as well, as many people told her she was very much like her father and the other Blairs.

Her father had a little tuft of hair at the crown of his head that would not stay down. Her mother was always wetting it to make it stay in place any time they went somewhere. It was almost a wasted effort, for as soon as the hair dried, it popped right back up again. Shane had that same bit of hair that wouldn't stay in place. It was forever standing up. It almost looked as though it was a family trait.

They sat there for a few minutes, and then she started to talk. She told him about her first meeting with Colin and how she'd felt intimidated by him. He was such a handsome man and seemed so confident. He made her feel like a young girl again and not sure of herself. As she got to know him that feeling passed.

She told Shane that Colin was really a very nice person. He was pleasant and easy to work with and quite helpful. He was an excellent pianist, and although he had never seen the piece they were about to play, it took him very little time to play along with her, and they played as though they had known the piece all their lives. When it came to music, they seemed to have a common bond and playing together was very natural for them. The more she worked with him, the better she liked him, and she felt he liked her too.

She sat still for a moment or two, and Shane stayed where he was, saying nothing. He wanted to let her talk and get it out of her system. He knew that sometimes talking was the only way to relieve the pressure and let it all out.

Ann continued on with her story. She told Shane about Colin's sincerity when speaking about his marriage, and the love and adoration he felt for his wife and two children. They were the joy of his life. They *were* his life. He was an honest man. However, that did not help her. The more she saw of him, the more she cared for him.

With her voice low and full of feeling, she told Shane how she had learned he had feelings for her as well, and how they had spent the last two days there together and had made a tape of some of their playing, along with Colin singing and playing guitar.

Shane let her talk as long as she needed. She told him that it had been a good trip and a great experience, and that, even though it had ended on a sad note, the time they had spent together had been some of the most memorable of her life and she would live it again if she was asked to.

The worst part was having to part knowing they would probably never see each other again. She told Shane that nothing in her life had ever hurt more than that. Colin was a real love in her life, and he belonged to someone else. She said she just hoped his wife realized how lucky she was and what a terrific man she had.

They sat for a while longer in silence before Ann sat up and looked at Shane.

"I don't suppose you can relate to that story, but thank you for listening."

"Ann, you're wrong. I can relate to that story. I have a similar one, and I've never told anyone about it. It hurt so much, and I didn't have anyone to tell it to other than my parents, and I just couldn't do that, so I kept it to myself. It hurt for a long time, and it still does if I let it, but I just tucked it away as an experience."

"Do you want to talk about it?" asked Ann. "I'm a good listener too, and anything you tell me will never go any further."

Shane started to talk. He told her that it had happened when he was in London, England, doing research for a novel he was writing. He was visiting a large teaching hospital in Whitechapel, when he met a student nurse. She was taking him throughout the facility and telling him about it. She was about to graduate at the end of that term. She was married to a naval officer who was away at sea.

"I spent a couple hours with her at the hospital. As I went to leave, she was putting on her coat. She said she was finished for the day, so I asked her if she would like to go for a cup of tea and she agreed. It was similar to you and Colin. We got to talking and found we had many interests in common. We talked for a long time, and it was almost seven o'clock in the evening before I noticed the time.

"I told her I was going to a restaurant for dinner, hopefully nearby, and asked her if she would like to join me. She did, and we talked for another couple of hours. It was almost as if we had known each other all our lives. She was a beautiful young woman and certainly had all the qualities you'd expect of a nurse, kind, patient, and compassionate."

He sighed. "I was in England for about six weeks, and we continued to see each other. She told me she loved her husband and how much she missed him when he was at sea, sometimes for six to eight months. I was aware that there was no future for us, but I just couldn't bring myself to let go. I had the feeling she was starting to care for me the same way I cared for her, but I didn't want to be the one to come between two people who loved each other.

"So I ended the trip. She saw me off at the airport. I gave her a hug and a kiss on the cheek. There were tears streaming down her cheeks. I picked up my belongings and almost ran down the ramp to my plane, before she saw that I was about to cry too. It was just like you said. It was one of the most difficult things I ever had to do, and I will never forget it. I'll never forget her. At that time, at least, I believed she was the love of my life. It hurt and sometimes it still does."

They sat there for a few more minutes, each lost in their own thoughts. Finally, Shane stood up, and she quickly followed. It was getting close to noon, and they decided it was time to go home before someone came looking for them. Ann had not told her parents where she was going and neither had Shane. They rode home and parted in the driveway, agreeing to meet again in the morning by the river.

Ann spent most of the summer in Guysborough, where she and Shane sat on the beach and talked or rode their bikes here and there throughout the county, viewing every nook and cranny that caught their attention. They talked about anything that came to mind. On one occasion, the topic of the piece of music written by Ann's great-grandfather came up. Shane's great-grandmother, Mary Morgan, had the same piece of music. Shane had found it in one of her music books that had been passed down to him. The question was, how did she get that piece of music? Was there a connection here? Did they know one another?

During one of these conversations, Ann remembered her father saying that she should take another look inside the old violin case. She hadn't thought of the old case in a long time. She made a mental point of checking it out the next time she was home. Perhaps there was more there. If there was, her great-grandfather certainly had a mysterious way of giving the family his history.

Was there something he would just as soon no one knew or did he believe that the one who found all his information would care for his violin?

He chose wisely, as Ann was the one who uncovered his precious papers and she *did* look after his violin and had learned to play it. She carried on his talent and his tradition. He would have been very happy about that.

Summer passed all too quickly and the first of September found Ann back at school. Her classes were larger than usual for this term and the workload was time consuming, but once she got started and got to know her students, the load seemed lighter. She was involved with many of her students' extracurricular activities as well, and this took up even more of her time. However, she loved her job, and this was not a problem for her.

On one weekend in late September, Ann decided to do a little extra cleaning. There was a coat hanging in the closet in the back entry, and Ann decided to put it in the hall closet since she probably wouldn't be wearing it again until next spring. She hung the coat up, and that's when she noticed the old violin case and remembered what her father had said.

She took the case out and put it on the kitchen table. She opened it and found the tear in the red lining, where she had found the various papers. She slid her hand back into the opening and down the space between the case and the lining. She moved it around the area. At first, she felt nothing. She was about ready to give up when her hand struck something. It seemed to be another piece of paper. It was almost like tissue paper, seemingly very fragile, so Ann was very careful.

No wonder I missed it before, she thought. She couldn't get a firm hold on it. It seemed so delicate she was afraid to apply much pressure and ruin it. There was only one thing to do: remove the lining far enough back to allow her to see what was there before she removed it. She very carefully began to loosen the red lining.

It held securely at first but suddenly let go and came away from the case. She pulled it away, leaving just a little bit of it fastened so she would know where to put it back, if she decided to do so at some point.

"Aha," she muttered. "What have I here?"

She unfolded the thin paper very carefully, and as she did, she could see that there was some writing on it, quite faint but readable. She looked at it closely, it read, "Susan Morgan, Born May 12, 1935, daughter of Mary Morgan and Alex Blair."

Ann stood and stared at the paper. It took her a few seconds to recognize the name "Mary Morgan." Then it came to her. That was the name on the piece of music Shane had—the name of his great-grandmother!

She and Shane had the same great-grandfather: Alex Blair! They were related! That would explain why he always seemed like a relative to her, and why he had some of the same characteristics as her father. If the truth were known, he too was a Blair. His great-grandfather's musical talents were carried on through him, as well as through Ann. Apparently, his great-grandmother was musical as well, so he got his talent from both sides of the family.

Ann sat down. This was quite a find, shedding more light on the life of Alex Blair. Grammie did not have this bit of information for her write up. Or did she? Perhaps she had an inkling of what had happened in his life and why he'd ended up in Guysborough, but hadn't wanted to divulge that part of the story.

Was Ann's great-grandmother still living when he was with Mary? She would have to find out the date when Margaret, her great-grandmother, passed away. Apparently, there was more to this story than she had anticipated. She almost felt like she was playing detective. She couldn't wait to tell her parents and her grandmother.

She couldn't wait to tell Shane! She and Shane were related, which explained why she had sometimes thought of him as a brother or a cousin from the time they first met. She wondered if he thought of her in the same way.

Ann turned back to the case. The piece of paper she had retrieved was not the only paper there. Another piece of paper was glued to the bottom of case. She very carefully removed it from its resting place. It was a map. Ann carried the paper to a chair near a lamp in the living room and sat down. She carefully surveyed it. It looked like a map of the area where her house was in Guysborough. It had a large dot on it, and printed beside the dot were the words "my other cabin."

There was a line from the cabin, which Ann felt was the driveway she travelled on every time she visited her home there. The line crossed Shane's driveway and went farther into the woods. She became a little lost from there. She didn't remember seeing another road branching off his driveway. After a few minutes, she gathered up both papers and put them in her purse. She wanted to show them to her parents and Shane. Perhaps Shane had noticed another road or path leading off his driveway. Or maybe the road had only been a path and was now grown over.

This old case has been hiding a lot of information over the years, she thought, as she closed it and carried it back to the closet. She had just discovered some more mysteries. Her first task now was to find the date her great-grandmother Margaret had passed away. Was it after 1935? Was she still alive when Susan was born? Was Alex Blair having an affair with Mary Morgan? There were so many questions with no answers, but she was sure she could find them.

Ann pondered these new pieces of information for a few minutes. *As far as my family is concerned, this is unknown family history. I think it should be shared with them.* She rushed to the phone and called her mother. There was no answer. She called her house in Guysborough and found they were there. They exchanged salutations, and then Ann told her mother that she had checked the inside of the old violin case, as her father had asked her to do, and had found some more information that seemed to be very important.

"Do you mind if I pick up Grammie and we come down for the night?" she asked.

"Of course not! We'd love to see both of you."

"Mom, I think this information also involves the Robertsons. Are they at their place?"

"Yes, they are," answered her mother. "I think Shane is there as well."

"Yes, I knew he was home. We keep in touch," Ann said. "I will call Grammie, pick her up, and we'll be there in a couple of hours."

The drive with Grammie was pleasant, and soon they were driving up the driveway of her Guysborough residence. Bill and Barbara were there, and as soon as they entered the house, they could smell dinner was cooking. The aroma spread throughout the whole place.

They had some family chit chat, and when dinner was over and the dishes washed and put away, they settled in the living room.

"Let's call the Robertsons and ask them to join us," Ann ventured. "I think they should be in on this as well." They all agreed and Barbara made the call.

WITHIN HALF AN HOUR, Shane and his parents were there. Hesitation never presented itself when they were asked to visit the Blairs. Tom and Elsie sat with the others in the living room, while Ann and Shane shared a few private moments in the kitchen before joining them. Barbara and Bill opened a bottle of wine and poured some for each one of them.

After some idle conversation, Ann took over. She told them that her father had asked her to check the old violin case one more time, just to see if there was any more information there. She said that she had and had found two notes that she felt were written by her great-grandfather. She produced the one about the birth of Susan Morgan, born May 12, 1935, father Alex Blair, mother Mary Morgan.

When the name Mary Morgan was mentioned, everyone looked stunned. The wheels started to turn. Mary Morgan was Shane's great-grandmother. Alex Blair was Ann's great-grandfather. The two families were related. Shane and Ann had the same great-grandfather: Alex Blair.

Alex Blair had two sons with Margaret, his wife: George (Grammie's husband) and Herbert. Mary Morgan had one daughter, Susan, who was Shane's grandmother. Susan and George (Ann's grandfather) were half siblings, making Shane's father and Ann's father half first cousins, and Shane and Ann half second cousins. They sat there speechless for a few minutes letting this all sink in.

Finally, Shane said, "Isn't it strange that both families, who had no idea they were connected, moved to Guysborough and lived side by side? It makes me wonder why. I've often heard it said that everything happens for a reason. I never really thought much about it until now. There must be a reason. Maybe fate has stepped in here."

As he said this, he looked over at Ann. Was she the reason in his life? He was hoping so, but time would tell.

Grammie was taking this all in. She didn't know all the details but was suspicious that there was still something in Alex Blair's life that the family was unaware of. She remembered that Margaret, Alex's wife, had passed away in 1937, two years after Susan was born. Apparently, Alex was having a little fling on the side, and the situation had gotten away from him.

At this point, Grammie began to shift around in her chair. They all knew she had more to add to the story, and she was ready to do so.

"As some of you know," she said, "Alex spent his last year or so with my husband George and me. He often talked to me, but I was never to tell anyone else what he told me, and I promised I wouldn't. However, most of what he told me, you now know, so I don't feel I'm betraying him when I fill in some of the details of what I know of his story.

"Susan was born in Boston. Her mother was living there at the time.

She stayed there until after Margaret had passed away. That's when Alex went looking for a place for them to stay away from gossips. He had a friend from Nova Scotia. The friend knew of a small cabin in Guysborough where no one would know them. Alex bought the cabin, and they lived there together until Susan was about eighteen years old.

"At around that time, Susan met David Robertson. He was a travelling salesman at the time, working for the Watkins Company. She married him, and they moved to Halifax. This was around 1955.

"After Susan left, Mary and Alex moved to Toronto, where he worked in a music store and taught violin lessons. Mary taught piano lessons at their home. Mary passed away in 1965, leaving Alex alone. He didn't like it there by himself, so he packed up his belongings and moved back to the cabin in Guysborough. He was only there for about a year when he got sick.

"That was when he moved in with George and me. He only lived with us for a year or two when he passed away. He was in his late seventies at the time. He left his belongings at my place, and that's how I happened to have his old violin, the one that Ann has now. I am afraid that's all I know about his life. He was a good man and a very talented one, and perhaps with the film Ann took part in, he will get a little bit of the fame he deserved. But I don't think the world has to know the story of the last years of his life."

The other five people sat there, completely taken in by Grammie's story. They'd had no idea their lives were intertwined. They were related. However, there was still some mystery involved here. What had brought the Robertson family to Guysborough, and especially to the same area? Why were they now living side by side and partly using the same driveway?

"Are we missing something here? I still don't understand how we ended up here together" Shane piped up.

"I think if we pool our knowledge and thoughts, this should be fairly easy to solve," Ann added. At that point, she decided they'd all had enough family history for one evening, and that she would keep the map to show Shane when they were alone.

After a cup of tea and some of Barbara's oatcake, the Robertsons left. They all agreed to think about what they had learned this evening and would go back in the family archives to see if they could add to the information they now had. Shane wanted to spend some alone time with Ann. He stayed for another hour or so, kissed Ann, and left for home. His feelings for her deepened every time he saw her.

Ann was back to work on Monday morning and with her teaching, music lessons and housekeeping the time passed.

Grammie was also busy but with a very different activity. She was determined to find out how the Robertsons' second home happened to be next to Ann's house in Guysborough. She was great at cutting out newspaper articles that she felt were of significance to the family and filing them away.

She dug out all her old clippings and settled down to read them. She was sure there would be something there that would lead her to the answer. It took her some time to unfold all the articles and read them.

She sorted them as she went. There were some that would be no help to her whatsoever. The ones she was sure were of some use she put into another pile.

She was at the task for an hour or more when she came across an article from one of the Guysborough papers. She unfolded the article and read it. The information was not very long in content. It simply stated that a new cottage was being built on the Old Guysborough Road by a couple by the name of Tom and Susan Robertson. It mentioned the fact that Susan was brought up on an adjoining property and loved the area. The information ended there. She set the clippings down and thought for a few minutes.

She was trying to remember if Alex had ever mentioned this fact or if he had even known. She figured he must have; otherwise she didn't know why she would have cut out the article in the first place. She refolded the clipping and immediately put it in her purse for her next trip to Guysborough. At least she would have some information to help with the mystery of the house and land owned by the Robertson family in the area.

The time flew by very quickly for Ann, and Thanksgiving was upon her before she knew it. She packed a few things, locked her house, picked up Grammie, and drove to Guysborough. Bill and Barbara were already there, and as always, the smell of dinner cooking met her as they entered the house. Ann loved this place. In fact, the whole family was happy to spend time together here. It was a comfortable, cozy house with a great view, giving one a place to just sit and forget all their cares. Ann was happy here. The whole family felt at peace here, even Grammie.

On the Saturday evening, the Blairs invited the Robertsons to their home for dinner. After some idle chit chat, the subject of how the Robertsons' home happened to be next to the Blair property came up. At this point, Grammie produced the clipping she had found. As Shane's father John read it, he didn't seem all that surprised.

"I think I can fill in the rest of the story," he said. "My parents, Tom and Susan Robertson, never ever talked about family history, so I don't know very much about their early days together. They were married for about ten years before they had any children. They were afraid they weren't going to have any when my sister, Ruth, came along. She's eleven years older than I am.

"We don't know much about the early lives of our parents. As far as Ruth and I can figure out, when our parents had children to look after, they felt they no longer had any use for the cabin, so they advertised it for sale. It was bought by an American couple. The couple who bought it did nothing with it, so they eventually advertised it for sale as well, and that is where we come in.

"Shane was looking for a quiet place where he could write without being disturbed. A friend of his saw the advertisement in the paper. He knew Shane was searching for a quiet place, and he told him about it. Shane visited the cabin and thought it was just what he was looking for, so he bought it. We didn't look into the history of the place or realize we had any part in that story."

"If it was only a small cabin when Shane bought it," Bill said, "how did it get to be the gorgeous property it is today, if all Shane wanted was a place to write?"

"Shane only spends part of his time here," John said. "He travels for a good part of the year. Elsie and I loved the nice setting up here overlooking the river, and with Shane's permission, we built it to what you see now. The only stipulation was that we must leave the place to him when he's working on a novel. He wants peace and quiet when he's writing. When he's here writing, we are not."

They all sat in silence for a few minutes. Each one of them seemed to be letting the story of how they happened to live side by side, and the fact that they were family, sink in.

"It's a small world," said Grammie. "People who are meant to be together should be together. All family members should be there for each other. It just took you a little while to find each other. The Lord works in mysterious ways. I knew Alex Blair fairly well, and I'm sure he's looking down and smiling now that you're finally united. It took some time, but the main thing is that it's happened. Now it's up to us to see that we're always here for each other and help one another whenever the need arises. It is my wish that our friendships grow, and we will always enjoy our time together."

"Amen to that. Words of wisdom, I am sure," John said.

The remainder of the evening passed with Ann on the violin and Shane at the piano, playing some of their favourite pieces while the others enjoyed a glass of wine, and Grammie opted for a cup of tea.

They played Alex Blair's piece of music, and now they were almost certain that Mary Morgan's name should be added to the composition. All too soon, it came time to part. As they went out the door, Elsie announced that she was cooking Christmas dinner and the Blairs were invited.

"Oh, that is so nice! Now I have something to look forward to when I go back to work on Monday," exclaimed a smiling Ann.

The rest of the year passed without too much ado, and time went by as expected. The Blairs spent Christmas with the Robertsons. Ann and Shane kept in contact with each other and played the violin and piano together whenever they got the chance. They both had the same love for playing, and the more they played together, the better they sounded. It was obvious they both had a gift for music and were very talented.

The winter passed without incident, and Easter was spent at home as there had been a big snowstorm and the roads were not good for travelling. Soon the end of the school term was in sight, and the usual preparations for the end of the term were in progress. Ann was busy with all the usual tasks, and soon the last day of the school term arrived and she was able to take a few days and just relax.

Cleaning and catching up on some work at home took up a few days, and soon Ann was ready to do some of the things she had been looking forward to all through the school term. As soon as these were completed, she was off to Guysborough and some relaxation.

Shane had just finished his latest book and decided to take some time away from writing to refresh his mind. They took a few road trips on their bicycles and visited many of the little places along the shores of Guysborough County and the surrounding area. They were almost convinced they had visited more places in the county than the people who had lived there all their lives.

They spent some afternoons at Shane's place playing music, which was something they loved to do. They liked being together and since most of their interests were the same, there was never a shortage of things to do. The families often had dinner or lunch at one of their homes, and music was always part of that time together.

Life Goes On

THE SUMMER WAS SLIDING to an end, and the school year was soon starting again. Ann loved her teaching job, but her days at her home away from home were precious to her, and she was not looking forward to them ending. However, she had no say in the matter and very soon she would be back.

The first day of school found Ann in front of her homeroom class. This year, she had a grade-ten class as her homeroom. She was teaching grades ten and eleven mathematics this term, and as usual, her load was a heavy one. Every class had at least thirty-five students, and she had five classes of them.

Altogether, she had over one hundred and eighty students, and each class had students of all levels, which made the job an even bigger task. She had also taken on many extracurricular activities, so she was in for a busy year.

The first weeks of the school year passed very quickly, and with her heavy workload and her music, before she knew it, Thanksgiving weekend had arrived. She was looking forward to the couple days of change and knew Shane would be there and they could do some cycling together.

It was not really cold out, but there was a nip in the air and there was the likelihood of some frost through the night. Ann called Shane, and they talked for some time about all that had happened since they had last seen each other. They agreed to meet the next morning around nine o'clock at the place where their driveways met.

The following day dawned bright and warm for the time of year. Ann was out of bed early, ate some breakfast, had a quick shower, and was off down the driveway to meet Shane. He was there waiting for her when she arrived. After a warm hug, they were on their way for a day of exploring. They traveled to Boylston and took Route 344 around the shore through Medford and on to Mulgrave. Then they went across country to Upper Big Tracadie, through to Monastry, and back to Boylston. They had made the complete circle and enjoyed every minute of the journey.

It had been a busy day and now that it was coming to an end, they decided to go to the little restaurant in Guysborough and get some dinner before they went on home.

The restaurant was busy when they arrived and they had to wait for some time before dinner was served to them. This gave them some time to discuss their day's travels. They both felt it was nice to see as much of the county as possible, and what better way to do that than by bicycle? They ate heartily and then pedalled on home. Shane left her at the juncture in the driveway, but before he did, he got off his bike and gave her a kiss and a warm hug.

He lingered longer than usual, and Ann found she did not mind one little bit. There was no doubt that she really liked Shane. The thing that really stopped her from thinking differently of him was the fact that they were related, even if they were only half second cousins. They did have the same great-grandfather but different great-grandmothers. They finally parted and said goodnight, promising to meet the next day. Shane said he would call her, and they would set something up. She drove on to the house just as darkness approached.

The next day was Sunday, and the family slept late. When everyone appeared on the scene, it was too late for breakfast so they had brunch. Ann and Barbara prepared a delicious meal of muffins, sausages, bacon and eggs with fruit, orange juice, and coffee. They enjoyed their time together, and the conversation was light and pleasant. When the meal was over, Ann and her mother cleaned up, and then they all retired to the living room, where Bill had the fireplace ablaze. They settled for a quiet afternoon.

Ann stayed for a while and then left to make her bed and tidy up her bedroom. She checked to see if Grammie had made her bed. Of course, she had. Grammie always made her bed as soon as she got up. As she headed back to her room, her cell phone rang. It was Shane. He wanted to know if she would like to go for a drive. She said she would. She never refused a chance to be with Shane, and it was a good afternoon to go out for a little while.

Of late, she really looked forward to the times she spent with Shane. He was so pleasant to be with, and he also seemed to enjoy the times they were together. She missed these times together when she was away at school, or he was off on one of his trips in search of material for a novel he was working on.

Shane drove up to the house to get her within the hour, and they were off for an afternoon of exploring. They had no particular destination planned, just being with one another was enough.

They stopped in the little park in Boylston and walked around it and then sat on a bench in the sunshine. It was an unusually warm day for October so they took advantage of one of the last warm days before the colder weather set in. Shane talked about the novel he was presently writing, and Ann about her school duties. Each one was interested in what the other was doing, and when they approached these subjects, there was much to talk about.

It was starting to get chilly and Ann shivered. Shane moved closer and slipped his arm around her. Ann started to realize that she was beginning to have real feelings for Shane. She cared a great deal for him. And why wouldn't any girl care for him? He was a handsome, talented, intelligent, thoughtful, and kind man, and it was obvious that he cared for her. She slipped an arm around him, and they sat there without speaking for some time, just enjoying the time and place.

Eventually, they looked at each other, and he kissed her. Then they were locked in each others' arms and kissed again. Ann realized she was falling in love with him. As for Shane, he had known he loved Ann from almost the first time they met. He was the type of person who believed in not rushing things.

Shane knew how he felt, and he had planned to wait and see what happened. He had fallen for the wrong woman once and did not want to be hurt that way again. Since she had fallen for the wrong man before too, he didn't want her to be hurt that way again either. It was his decision to let matters take their course. They sat there and neither one said a word. Finally, they got up, walked toward the car, and drove off.

Shane drove up to the Blair house, and Ann invited him in. They talked to the family for a while and then Shane decided that, if their first love was for one another, then their second was their music. Ann picked up her violin, which was always on the piano when she was in Guysborough, and Shane seated himself at the piano, and they played.

They entertained the family for some time and ended with their favourite piece, which their great-grandfather had named "The Old Violin." It seemed an appropriate selection, since it had connected the two families. The evening was getting late, and Shane decided it was time to go home. Ann walked with him to his car, and they kissed goodnight.

THANKSGIVING DAY DAWNED WITH the sun out but with some white frost on the ground, the first of the fall season. It was a friendly reminder that colder weather was on the way. They had a late breakfast, and three o'clock found the Robertsons entering the Blairs' home, laden with dessert for after the dinner.

The delicious smell of dinner cooking was everywhere, and the men settled in the living room close to the fireplace with Grammie and Ann, while Barbara and Elsie made the finishing touches to the meal. The two women said they wanted to be left alone, as too many women in the kitchen would only be a stumbling block to production. Ann and Grammie were quick to agree and let them be.

Dinner was at four o'clock sharp. Grammie said Grace, and everyone enjoyed a delicious meal topped with Barbara's homemade apple pie and coffee. Even though everyone was reluctant to part, Ann, Grammie, John, and Elsie all had to be home and up early the next morning, so they had to excuse themselves and leave.

Bill and Shane promised to help Barbara clean up and that made Ann feel better, as she really wanted to help her mother with the work, but she insisted Ann get on the road before it was late. Besides, she also had to get Grammie home and settled. Shane walked Ann to her car and promised to call her later. Ann drove home without incident and made sure Grammie was all settled in before she went on to her own house.

Shane called Ann around nine thirty, and they talked for some time. He assured her that he and her father had stayed with Barbara until the cleanup from dinner was complete. His present book was going to keep him busy for the next month or so, and his parents were going back home to give him quietness to work.

"I love you, Ann, and I will always have you in my heart," he said. "I'm looking forward to the next time we're together. I'll make a trip up your way in a week or so. I am so looking forward to that."

"I love you too," she answered, "and I look forward to seeing you very soon. Good luck with the book, and don't work too hard. Every once in a while, take a walk to the river. You'll find it will clear your mind so you can work better. I know that works for me. I'll call soon."

Ann hung up the phone with an empty feeling. She had seen him only a few hours ago, but she missed him already. She made sure she had everything ready for the next day, took a warm bath, and went to bed. She fell asleep with thoughts of the past three days and the pleasant hours she had spent with Shane.

The Unexpected

THE MONTHS OF OCTOBER and November passed quickly. Ann's workload was heavy, and she was involved with many of the extracurricular activities, especially with the year's graduating class. Shane came to visit her when he had the opportunity. Time was of an essence for him as well. He had a novel that was to be completed by the middle of December.

Ann looked forward to the times Shane came to be with her. She purchased a large keyboard for her home, and whenever they were together, there was always music. They were definitely two of a kind when it came to music, and they played together with so much pleasure that it was plain to see it would always be part of their lives.

Christmas was fast approaching, and this time it was the Blairs who were having the Robertsons over for the meal. Plans were in the works, and it looked as though everything was going as planned. Then disaster struck.

It was two weeks before Christmas. Shane spent the weekend with Ann, but he had to be home for the next day. A big snowstorm was forecast for the area. Shane decided he had better leave earlier than planned. Ann wanted him to stay and go home on the Monday morning, but he was afraid the roads would not be plowed in time for him, so he decided to leave and try to beat the storm. As he went out the door to leave, snowflakes were in the air and the wind was picking up. Ann had a feeling of dread as she watched him wave to her and drive off.

After Shane left, Ann made herself a cup of tea and settled down to catch up on her work for the next day at school. She was busy for an hour or so when she looked out the window and saw a raging blizzard outside. Her heart skipped a beat. She could not believe the storm had come up so fast.

Where was Shane? Was he ahead of the storm or in the middle of it? If it was snowing and blowing as hard where he was as it was here, she was sure he would not even be able to see the road. He would be in grave danger. She did not want to phone him as it would take his attention off the road. She'd just have to sit and wait and pray.

Three hours went by, and she still had not heard from him. The Robertsons were at their home so there was no one at Shane's place, and her parents were at home as well. She did not want to phone them and set them to worrying also. She turned the radio on to the New

Glasgow station. There was nothing on except some annoying music. She left the radio on that station for some time. Finally, the news came on and the first item broadcast was about an accident in Marshy Hope. A car had gone out of control and had side swiped a tractor trailer. The driver was injured and had been transported by ambulance to the hospital in New Glasgow. He was being prepared for air ambulance to the hospital in Halifax.

Ann started to cry. She had a feeling that the injured driver was Shane. She paced the floor. She had to talk to someone, but she didn't want to worry someone else if it was a false alarm. She waited and listened to the radio to see if she heard any more news on the driver. As she listened, she paced the floor and continually looked out the window. The storm was raging so badly that she could see nothing outside, just snow.

Finally, she could stand it no longer. She decided to call her parents. Her mother answered the phone. Barbara told her the storm was a full-blown blizzard there.

"Oh, Mom, I am so worried. Shane left here for Guysborough just as the storm was starting. I wanted him to stay, but he said he had to be home for Monday. There was an accident in Marshy Hope. It happened just about the time Shane would be in that area. I heard it on the radio. It said the driver was taken to New Glasgow and was being prepared for the trip to the Victoria General Hospital in Halifax."

"Now, Ann, you don't know for sure it was Shane in that accident. Stop worrying. Shane is used to driving in these conditions. It may not have been him. Let's just hope it wasn't. I know you're worried and so are we. But let's just wait and see. We will keep our ears peeled for any news, and if we hear any, we'll be in touch. Now, pull yourself together, and just wait and see. I will talk to you later. Bye."

The phone call to her mother did not make Ann feel much better, and she continued to pace the floor. There was no sense in going to bed, as she wouldn't be able to sleep. She turned the dial on the radio to the Antigonish station, and the news there was the same as she'd heard on the New Glasgow station. If only Shane had listened to her and stayed until the storm was over! Men were so stubborn sometimes. *They think they can brave through anything.*

The evening passed with no word from Shane or on Shane. Ann wanted to call his parents but didn't want to worry them. Perhaps he was all right and had stopped somewhere to be safe until the storm subsided. She had to think these things just to keep her sanity. It had now been about nine hours since he had left her place, and he should have been home long ago. If he were home, he would have phoned her. Then again, there was quite a wind with the storm, and his phone might be out.

"What am I thinking?" she said out loud. "He has a cell phone."

She kept listening to the radio to see if there was any more news on the crash. Nothing had come through since the first message she'd heard a few hours ago. She was almost frantic. There was no one to talk with. She was alone. She could call her mother again, but she was sure that, if her mother heard anything, she would call her. There was nothing on the radio but music. She would listen to the news at midnight, she decided. It would be on soon.

Ann sat down in her favourite chair. She almost dozed off when the sound of the news announcer broke in. The first item on the news was the traffic accident in Marshy Hope. He announced that the cause of the accident was bad driving conditions. A car crash had caused the driver of the car to be air lifted from the New Glasgow Hospital to the Victoria General Hospital with severe injuries. It was a male driver, but the name would not be released until the family was informed. There would be more information announced as it became available.

Ann sat there completely stunned. She could just feel that it was Shane. A few minutes later, the phone rang. It was her mother. She sounded like she was crying.

"Brace yourself, Ann!" she said. "It *was* Shane in the accident. Elsie just called me. He has a broken leg, several broken ribs, and a dislocated shoulder. He got a very bad smash on the head and is in a coma. He's in the V.G. right now. They were lucky to get him there in this storm. Why on earth would he get out on the roads on a day like this?"

"I tried to get him to stay here," answered Ann, "but he said he had to be home for tomorrow. I have no idea what was so important that he had to be in Guysborough for tomorrow. As soon as this storm lessens, I'm on my way to Halifax. There'll be no school tomorrow, but even if there is, I won't be there."

"Wait for us," her mom said. "As soon as the roads are reasonably safe, we're on our way there as well. I'm sure John and Elsie will be on their way there too. Don't go anywhere until you hear from us. I'll call just as soon as I have any news."

As soon as Ann hung up the phone, she started to cry. Why hadn't she insisted Shane stay until the roads were safe? If she had made a point of it, she was sure he would have listened to her. The thing was that the storm came up so suddenly that it was difficult to tell it was going to get so bad, so fast. She started to pace the floor again. Then suddenly she stopped.

She went to her bedroom, packed a small bag with a few necessary clothes, and put some toiletries out on the counter in the bathroom, so they would be handy for the morning. She took a quick shower and pulled on her pyjamas and housecoat. Then she curled up in her favourite chair, knowing that going to bed was of no use. There was no way she was going to sleep. She sat there waiting for the phone to ring again, and at the same time, she was terrified at what the news might be. Around two o'clock in the morning, she dozed off and put in the remainder of the night drifting in and out of sleep.

Finally, it was daylight. Ann got up and walked to the window. There was well over a foot of snow on the ground, and it had drifted into piles here and there. The road in front of her house had not been plowed yet. She listened to the radio. The forecast said the worst of the storm was over, but drifting snow was still a problem. Schools throughout the province were closed and it advised everyone concerned to keep listening as it was doubtful if there would be school the following day as well.

Ann made herself ready to face the day. She finished packing her bag as she knew that, at some time during the day, she was making the trip to Halifax. She ate some breakfast, and at around nine o'clock, she phoned her principal and told him the situation and asked if it would be all right if she took a few days off, if it was necessary. He said he would get a substitute teacher for her but told her to keep in touch with him. She thanked him and agreed to keep him up to date.

The morning was getting on, and Ann had not heard from anyone. She decided to call her mother to see if she had heard anything from the Robertsons. Her mother said that Elsie had phoned the hospital in Halifax, and they told her he was still in a coma. He had opened his eyes a few times though, which was good news. Barbara told her the roads in her area were being plowed now, and as soon as they were passable, Elsie and John would be on their way to Halifax. They would call her before they left and pick her up on the way down.

Ann paced the floor waiting for their call. Then she decided she had better call Grammie to see how she was and tell her about Shane before she heard it on the radio. Grammie said that she'd heard about the accident but didn't realize it was Shane.

"Don't worry, Grammie. I'm waiting for Shane's parents. I'm going to Halifax with them, but I'll keep you informed. Stay in the house. Don't go out in this snow. I'll be over to see you as soon as I get back. I love you. Bye."

It was another two hours before John and Elsie arrived. Ann grabbed her overnight bag and hopped in the back seat. She was so glad to finally be on her way. She was so anxious to see Shane, but she was afraid of what she might find when she did see him.

The roads were passable but not good, and it took them almost two hours to make the trip. Finding a place to park was a problem when they got there, so John let her out and she went in ahead of John and Elsie. She inquired from the main registry where he was and headed for Shane's room. The elevator seemed to be slower than usual, but finally, she was on the right floor. She followed the signs and reached his room.

She opened the door and walked in, then stood there in total shock. He was stretched out on the bed with a bandage around his head. His face had several cuts and bruises and was badly swollen. If she had not known it was Shane, she would have thought it was someone else. His left leg was in a cast, and she could not see all of it but knew his ribs on the left side were cracked, so they were strapped along with his left shoulder, which he had dislocated badly. His hands had several deep cuts and were swollen.

He lay there, seemingly lifeless, and it scared Ann so badly that she started to cry. She stared at him and thought she saw his eyelids move. She gently picked up his swollen hands and spoke to him. At first, there was no response. He was just very still. As John and Elsie arrived, she thought she saw his eyelids move again.

Elsie took one look at her son and immediately started to cry. Ann put her arm around her, and they both cried. His father just stood there and stared at him. Ann wondered what was going through his mind. She felt he was just too macho to cry, but she knew that if he were alone, he would have cried too.

The three of them stood beside his bed for several minutes. They said very little and just looked at him as he lay there. Once he turned his head in their direction, as though he realized there was someone in the room with him. Ann thought she saw his eyelids flicker again, but it happened so fast she wasn't sure.

Elsie and John sat with Ann for half an hour or so, and then they decided to go out for some lunch. They asked Ann to go with them, but she said she wasn't hungry. She would rather stay with Shane. Elsie said she would bring some lunch back to her, and then she and John left.

Ann pulled up a chair and sat by Shane's bed. He lay there, completely still. It was obvious he was in a deep sleep, yet every once in a while, his eyelids moved, and he moved his hands as though he was trying his best to come back to reality. Ann held one of his scared, swollen hands very gently. She knew they were hurting and did not want to enhance the pain. She could almost feel his pain, and she hurt with him. It made her realize just how much she loved him. Shane was always so happy and cheerful and Ann found it difficult to see him this way. She felt a lump in her throat.

The Robertsons returned a couple hours later and found Ann holding Shane's hand and fast asleep in her chair. She woke up when Elsie pulled a chair over to sit beside the bed near her. They had brought a meal and some coffee back for Ann. They knew she had not eaten all day, and the last thing they needed was for her to get sick. John pulled a small table over close to Ann, and Elsie spread out a nice hot dinner with apple pie for dessert, and poured some coffee into a cup they had brought back with them. Ann ate everything they supplied. She hadn't realized how hungry she was. Then she remembered she had not eaten much since Shane was with her on the weekend.

Later that afternoon, Ann's parents arrived, and they too were in shock when they first saw Shane. Barbara could not believe the man she was looking at was the handsome Shane she had seen only a few days ago. *How quickly things can change*, she thought. She stood there with tears streaming down her face.

Ann was surprised by her mother's reaction, and tears started to run down her own cheeks. Her mother's response to his condition made her realize just how much the family loved Shane. She hugged Barbara, and they both sat down next to his bed.

Ann and her parents sat with Shane until a nurse came in and told them they would have to leave, because the doctor was coming in to see how Shane was progressing and do some testing. They left and went down the hall to a room available for visitors. They sat there and said very little for a few minutes. Finally, Bill stood up and walked to the window. He looked out at the traffic below and then suddenly he turned back to his family.

"I know we are all feeling very bad for Shane, but it could be worse," he said. "Shane could have been killed. As it is, he's alive and I have a feeling he will be fine. He is a healthy, strong man, and he will get through this. Let's not go back in there feeling so down. Let's be thankful for what it is and hope for the best. I'm sure that's what Shane would want us to do."

Barbara stood up and joined him. "Bill is right," she said. "Christmas is only a short time away. We will plan as we always do, and I know that, if possible at all, Shane will be sitting at the Christmas dinner table with us."

Bill and Barbara both sat down, and for some reason, everyone seemed to feel better. They just had to have a little faith and trust in God. Shane had some bad days to get through, but he would be fine soon. This thought seemed to make Ann feel somewhat better. She walked back down the hall to see if the doctor was still in Shane's room. She peeked in. The doctor was gone, but the nurse was still there tending to him. She cleaned his open wounds and bandaged one of them. Then she turned and saw Ann standing there.

"He seems to be resting comfortably," she said. "The doctor feels he'll open his eyes and come around soon. Just stay patient. I'll be in later to check on him." She turned and left.

Ann sat on the chair by Shane's bed. She gently picked up his hand and was sure she felt him squeeze hers just a little. He knew she was there. She was sure of that. She looked at his bruised and swollen face, and the tears were not far away. Then she remembered what her father had said. *We must be thankful for what it is. It could be much worse.* She leaned over and laid her head on the side of his bed. Within a few minutes, she was sound asleep.

Elsie came into the room. She saw Ann with Shane. She walked over to the bed, and when she realized Ann was asleep, she tiptoed out of the room.

The next day was Tuesday. There still was no school across the province, but things were starting to get back to normal. The doctor told her he was sure Shane would come around within a day or so. Her parents and Shane's parents went home, and she was alone with Shane. She seldom left his side. She ate at the cafeteria and showered and brushed her teeth in Shane's bathroom. As long as she was near Shane, she was fine.

It was the last week before Christmas. There were only three teaching days in that week, so Ann went home to finish up before the holidays. She did not want to leave Shane, but she felt she had to go. She kissed him and held his still swollen hand before she left, and then stood at the door and looked at him.

"I love you, and I'll be back as soon as I can," she whispered, before she closed the door.

The two days passed very quickly. The third day was only part of a day. The buses went home early and Ann used the remainder of the day to finish her Christmas shopping. The next day, she was on the way back to the hospital to be with Shane. The trip was much faster now as the roads were clear. She drove her own car down, with the hope the driving would be just as good on her way back. She found parking was much easier now and was soon on her way to Shane's room.

She opened the door to his room and got a delightful surprise.

Shane was awake and propped up in bed. The intravenous lines had been removed, and he looked at her as she entered. It took him a second to realize who it was, but he did know her.

"Ann," he said.

"Oh, Shane, you're awake! I am so glad."

She rushed to his bed and kissed him on the cheek. "This is the best Christmas present I could possibly get. I am so happy for you," she exclaimed excitedly.

Ann noticed the swelling on his face and hands had gone down, and his cuts and bruises were on the mend. She was so happy there were tears in her eyes. Shane reached over and picked up her hand. He held it for a few seconds and then put his other hand on top of hers.

"I knew you were holding my hand, but I just couldn't bring myself to do anything or say anything. I had the feeling people were with me, but there didn't seem to be a way I could let you know. When I finally did come around and opened my eyes, there was no one in the room. The nurse really got a surprise when she came in and I said something to her."

"Do you remember everything that happened?" asked Ann.

"Some of it's starting to come back. I remember being with you before the accident, and you asked me to stay but I said I had to go. I did start out before the storm got bad, but it wasn't long before the area was a raging blizzard. I remember going past New Glasgow but the exits were very difficult to see. The farther I drove, the worse it seemed to get. I was quite a distance past New Glasgow when I saw this big eighteen-wheeler come up beside me. The car took a swerve, and I remember hitting it, and that is it. The next thing, I opened my eyes, and I was here. It took me a few minutes to focus on where I was. I wasn't really sure until a nurse came in and filled me in on a few details."

"You scared us so badly. When we first heard of the accident on the radio, we didn't know if you were involved. Even when we heard the driver of the car was taken to Halifax, we didn't know who it was. We held our breaths for a few hours, and when we knew it was you, we were so scared. We didn't know what your injuries were. The storm was almost over by dawn the next day, but the roads were impassable. We had to wait until the roads were opened up before we could come here. Oh, Shane, when I first looked at you, all I could do was cry. You looked so hurt, and I was helpless to do anything about it."

Ann sat on the edge of the bed. She just wanted to be near him, and he was holding her hand so tight it seemed he was afraid he would slip back to the way he had been for the past five days. He was so glad to have her beside him. She didn't want to pressure him, but she was anxious to know if he had regained all of his memories, which the doctor had warned them might be affected. She thought about it for a few minutes, and then she just had to ask.

"Did all of your memory come back?" she asked.

Shane looked puzzled. He tried to sit up a little more in the bed, but his cracked ribs hurt when he moved and the shoulder was a bit of a hindrance as well.

"I remember almost everything since I woke up, but my life before the accident is very hazy. If someone were to tell me I could drive home now, I think I would know how to drive, but I don't think I'd remember how to get there. I can't remember my home or what I did for a living. I am just so grateful that I recognized you and remember you. The doctor said it may take a little time for those other memories to come back. Perhaps, all of a sudden, something will trigger my mind and my memory will return. I hope so."

"It will, I'm sure," said Ann. "I am so glad you knew me. It's only a few days to Christmas, and the doctor says that, if things look all right, I will be able to take you home for Christmas."

"Good. I don't want to be here for Christmas day," Shane said. "I know that, if I am here, you would be here as well and that wouldn't be a good Christmas for either of us."

Shane continued to get stronger. He was finally able to get out of bed. He had to use crutches to get around though, and it took him a day or so to get used to them. His cuts and bruises were slowly disappearing and the swelling on his face and hands was all but gone. His memories of before the accident had not come back yet, but he said that, every once in a while, it seemed close, like it would only take one important thing in his life to bring it all back.

On the day before Christmas, he was released from the hospital and Ann drove him home to his house in Guysborough. Even the view from the top of the hill overlooking the river did not seem to help, but he did stop and take a good look at it as he got out of the car.

His mother and father were there when he arrived, along with Ann's parents. He looked at them and said hello, but didn't yet have any recollections of them. It upset his parents, but they didn't let him know that. They knew Christmas was the time of miracles and were sure he would recall everything soon.

Christmas day dawned bright and sunny, but it was a very cold day. The Blairs were having the Robertsons over for dinner, which was to take place at four o'clock. The family, including Grammie, were up early, and the first thing they did was open their presents, and then have breakfast. Barbara stuffed the turkey and had it in the oven in plenty of time to have it ready for dinner. Ann and Grammie peeled the vegetables, and Ann set the table, which was always her job when she was present.

The Robertsons arrived around three o'clock. Dinner would be ready on time, so they settled before the fireplace in the living room where they exchanged gifts. Shane managed with the help of his crutches but seemed very quiet. It was as though coming here made him more aware of his surroundings, but it also seemed like he was trying harder than ever to remember, looking for that one little thing that would bring everything back. This place seemed so familiar, even more so than his own home, but he couldn't figure out why.

They ate dinner at the appointed time, and as usual, it was delicious. Ann and Elsie helped Barbara with the cleanup, and they all settled back in the living room to enjoy the tree and all the Christmas trimmings.

Shane sat in a chair close to the window to watch the sky darken over the river. Ann stood beside him for a few minutes, and then Grammie asked her to play her violin, perhaps some Christmas carols. Ann walked to the piano where she always kept her violin when in Guysborough, made sure it was in tune, and started to play.

Shane turned in his chair when he heard her play and stared at her and then at the piano. He listened. Ann played several carols, and then she began to play the piece she'd found in the old violin case. She played it through. All at once, Shane struggled to get up, grabbed his crutches, and made his way to the piano. He pulled out the bench and sat down. Ann continued to play. He listened for another moment and then started to play along with her.

She changed to another piece of music, and he followed along. Grammie was ready to clap, and the other four were so happy when they heard him play that they were almost in tears. They were so glad to hear them. Ann stopped playing, set her violin down, and threw her arms around Shane.

"Oh, Shane," she said. "You remembered! You played as well as you ever could. We're all so happy to hear you play."

Shane looked at her and a wide smile spread across his face. He said nothing for a minute or two and then started to talk.

"I remember!" he exclaimed. "I knew today, when I walked into this house, that it has a very special meaning for me. I now know why. I spent many hours here playing the piano, while Ann played the violin, and as soon as she played that piece, it started to come back to me. I remember!"

The family was so happy for Shane that Elsie and Barbara rushed over to give him a hug. Grammie threw him a kiss.

"I knew he would remember," declared Grammie. "It just took a little time and something very important to him to make that happen. Keep playing you two. I love to hear you play."

They played several more pieces. The more they played, the bigger the smile on Shane's face got. Then, all of a sudden, Shane stopped playing and swung around on the piano bench.

"Are the stores open tomorrow?" he asked.

Everyone looked puzzled for a moment and Barbara answered. "I think they are. If not, they're definitely open the next day. Why? What's so important?"

"There's something I have to do," he answered. "We'll just leave it at that for now."

They spent the remainder of the evening talking and listening to Ann and Shane play. Around midnight, the Robertsons went home. Ann and Shane remained in the living room after the others left. They talked for some time with Shane explaining to Ann how everything was coming back to him.

He was so happy to have his memory back. "And to think, it was the old violin tune written by our great-grandfather that did it," he said. "It's just as though he was here looking after us."

Ann smiled. "Grammie was right. The Lord works in mysterious ways."

Finally, Shane decided he had better go home. Ann drove him to his house and made sure he got into the house with no problem. Then they kissed, and she left for home.

The next day was sunny and cold, but the roads were good. Shane made a few phone calls and then asked his father if he would drive him to Antigonish as he had to pick something up.

Chapter 17

The Late Christmas Gift

THE TRIP TO ANTIGONISH took about half an hour as the roads were good. Shane asked his father to stop in front of a jewellery store in the downtown area, and with the help of his crutches he managed to make his way into the store. His father offered to help him, but Shane insisted he could make it on his own. It took some effort on his part, but he made it inside the store.

John waited in the car until he returned. Shane came out about half an hour later, and as far as John could see, he had bought nothing. His father didn't ask any questions, and they returned home.

Following the trip to Antigonish, John and Elsie went home just to check on things, because they had been at Shane's for a few days. It was winter, and it was a cold spell of weather. They wanted to make sure the furnace was going and everything was in order. Shane was left alone for a few hours.

As soon as he was sure he would be by himself, he called Ann and asked her if she could come over. She said she would be right there. He had told her he was alone, and she feared something had happened to him. She quickly put on a coat and winter boots and was out the door, arriving at his place in less than ten minutes. She rushed out of her car, up the steps, and into the house, and was very relieved to see that Shane was sitting at the kitchen table, and with exception of the cast on his leg, he was fine.

"Thank goodness," she said. "I was worried you'd fallen and hurt yourself."

"I'm fine. I'm alone though, and I want to talk to you."

She was startled and a little worried. What did he want to talk about? Was he thinking of going away with a cast on his leg? She hoped not. He still had his last book to finish. It was supposed to be finished before Christmas, but that had gotten put on the back burner with the accident.

"Don't look so concerned. I want to ask you something—something I intended to ask you at Christmas, but ... it didn't happen. After I lost my memory, there was something very important I tried my hardest to remember, and it wouldn't come to mind. Then, all of a sudden, when you started to play the violin, it came back. It was the first thing I remembered.

"The day I left for home, even though there was a storm approaching, I left because I was to be in Antigonish that afternoon to pick up a very important item. I was to be there for four o'clock. Of course, I didn't make it. This morning, I made a call and found out the gentle-man had heard I was in the accident, so he'd held the item for me. Dad took me to Antigonish this morning, and I got it."

Ann looked puzzled and wondered if he was just imagining things. Was he hallucinating? Did the bump on his head do more damage than first thought? She walked over and sat down beside him.

Shane reached into his pocket and came out with a blue velvet box.

"I would get down on one knee, but in my condition, I'm afraid I couldn't get up again."

He took both her hands in his and looked her in the eyes for a few seconds.

"Ann Blair, I love you. Will you marry me?"

Ann's heart skipped a beat. There was nothing in the world she would rather be than Mrs. Shane Robertson.

"Yes," she said. "Yes, yes, yes."

Shane opened the blue velvet box and put the ring on her finger. It was the most beautiful ring Ann had ever seen and all that more pre-cious because it came from Shane. It was yellow gold with three large diamonds, and it fit her finger to perfection.

"I love it. It is so beautiful. How did you get the size so perfect?" Ann asked.

"Remember the day you were playing in the sand, and you took your ring off and set it on a stone? You said it was a little big and you were afraid it would slip off your finger. When you went to put it back on, you couldn't find it. Well, when you weren't looking, I slipped it into my pocket. I knew then I was going to ask you to marry me, and I needed it for sizing. So, I stole it … for a short time." He reached into his pocket and gave her the ring. "I'm sorry I stole it, but it was for a good cause."

"I didn't think about it again. So, you're forgiven," she said.

Ann and Shane talked for some time after she got the ring. They were both so happy. They were just enjoying the moment now. Plans for a wedding would come later.

"Come with me, and we'll go tell my parents," Ann said. "They'll be so happy. They love you, Shane, and to have you for a son-in-law will make them so pleased."

Ann got their coats, and Shane picked up his crutches. He was getting quite adept at handling them now, and Ann drove back to her place.

She burst into the house and waited for Shane. Then they removed their coats and walked into the living room where Bill, Barbara, and Grammie were seated by the fireplace. Ann couldn't hold her excitement any longer and rushed over to show her ring to her family. Barbara jumped up, all smiles, and gave Ann a hug. Then she rushed over and hugged Shane and welcomed him into the family.

"I guess, technically, you're already in the family, but that's so far in the distance."

Bill shook Shane's hand and congratulated him. He told him how happy he was to have him marrying his daughter. Grammie told them how happy she was for them too. Shane was beaming. He was so glad

Ann's family was in favour of their becoming husband and wife. John and Elsie came in to see the Blairs before going home and were over-joyed with the good news.

"This calls for a drink!" exclaimed Bill, and he produced a bottle of wine. Barbara left the room, returned with the wine glasses, and the two families that were soon to be one drank to the health and happi-ness of Ann and Shane.

Barbara and Bill were delighted the Robertsons had dropped in on their way home. It made it possible for the two families to share and enjoy the good news.

"I have nothing really prepared for supper," declared Barbara. "However, we have plenty turkey and ham left over from Christmas. I can make sandwiches. I have apple pie and lots of holiday sweets too. We want you folks to stay so we can have a meal together. Just give me a little time, and I'll have it ready."

Ann jumped up. "I'll help you, Mom."

"Thank you," Elsie said. "We'd love to stay, but only if I can help as well."

The three women disappeared into the kitchen, and the meal was soon on the table. After supper and the cleanup were completed, every-one returned to the living room for some wedding talk and music. It was a joyous evening, and as soon as the wedding date was set, there would certainly be many more similar evenings.

The remainder of the Christmas vacation passed quickly with Ann spending most of her time with Shane. His parents had gone back home, and he was left alone. He was getting very skilled with his crutches and could maneuver around on them quite successfully. As soon as Ann returned home, he went back to work on his book. It had been due before Christmas but the publishers made allowances for him due to the accident. As soon as things got back to normal, he went back to writing. He missed Ann, but they talked every evening and she agreed to stay away until he had finished his writing. By that time, the cast would be off and he could be back to walking on his own again.

The winter passed without incident. There were some snowstorms and a few days of icy roads but those are expected in Nova Scotia during the winter months. Shane made a few trips to Lawson Brook to visit Ann, and she in turn made a couple of trips to visit him.

During March break, the two families got together. The wedding was the big topic of conversation. Ann and Shane had set the date for June thirtieth of the following year. Shane had some travelling to do for two books he had to write, and Ann had to spend six weeks of summer school at Dalhousie University during the summer of this year. They wanted these things finished so they could take a longer honeymoon. Right now, it seemed like a long way off, but with their work schedule, they knew time would pass quickly and wedding preparations took time.

June was a busy time for Ann with the usual exams, marking, grading, graduation banquet, church service, and prom. When this was finished, she was exhausted. She then had to pack for her summer-school course and spend four weeks in Halifax. During this time, Shane was in Ireland getting information for his next book.

Ann was finishing the fourth week of her course when she had a free afternoon. She decided to take a walk through the Halifax Public Gardens. She wandered around for about an hour looking at the various flowers, shrubs, and trees. She saw a park bench and decided to sit for a few minutes. It was quiet, so she took out one of the math books she had with her. She had to do a critique on several math text-books for her course at summer school.

She was only there for a few minutes when she noticed some people across the way from her. It looked as though it was a family of mom, dad, and two children. The man was sitting down and the other three were standing as though they were about to leave. All she could see of the man was the back of his head and his shoulders. For some reason, it looked familiar.

Ann sat there and watched them. She could hear them discussing what they were going to do next. The two children wanted to go for a sail on the ferry across the harbour, and it seemed as though the mother did as well. The father said that he would just stay in the park and wait until they came back. Apparently, that's what was decided, because the woman and the two children left, and as they departed, Ann heard the man say he would just be around the gardens when they came back.

Ann sat there staring at him. He'd even sounded familiar when he spoke. He stood up and looked in her direction. He glanced at her, turned to leave, and then quickly turned back. She had the feeling he recognized her, and as he looked in her direction again, she knew exactly who he was. He was someone she'd never expected to see again: Colin Watson. He walked over to where she sat and stood in front of her.

"Colin," she said. "What are you doing here? This is such a surprise. I never expected to see you here."

"My wife, Ella, and I decided to take our children on a vacation to the East Coast of Canada for their summer break from school. We felt this was a good time of year to do it. I never expected to see you here either."

"I'm taking a summer-school course at Dalhousie University. I had an afternoon free of classes so I decided to do a little sight-seeing. Imagine the surprise I got when you stood up. I really didn't think our paths would ever cross again. I'm so happy to see you."

"Do you want to go for a cup of coffee where we can sit and talk? Ella and the kids won't be back for a few hours. I have some time to kill."

"Yes. That would be nice. There's a little restaurant not far from here," Ann responded.

They walked down the street side by side, each one was probably thinking about the last few minutes they had spent together. Were those old feelings coming back or had each one buried them in a little secret place in their heart, only to be remembered on rare occasions? Was this one of those occasions? Would old feelings come back to the surface and be renewed here? Only time would tell.

They found a small café, ordered coffee, and sat in a back booth. They talked catching each other up on their lives since they'd made the movie on Alex Blair. Colin noticed the diamond engagement ring on Ann's finger. He stared at it for a moment and then asked her when she was getting married.

"I'm marrying Shane Robertson next June. He's a writer and has a home next to the one Alex Blair left me. He's in Ireland right now doing research for a novel he's writing. Shane is a terrific person and not only is he a writer but a very good musician, a great pianist. We play together quite often. It's just as enjoyable as playing with you. I'm sure you would really like each other."

Colin was happy for her, simply because she seemed so happy talking about Shane and the fact that they were getting married in less than a year. However, deep in his heart, he felt a little disappointed. He still had feelings for Ann. If it were possible to have two loves in his life, Ann would be the other one. She was totally different from his wife, Ella, whom he loved dearly, but Ann had a personality totally different from anyone he had ever known. For that very reason, he could not get her out of his mind. Seeing her again had only enhanced his feelings for her. This encounter was going to make it more difficult to forget her. However, he could deal with it.

He loved his wife and two children and would never do anything to hurt them. Ann had found someone she loved and cared very deeply for, and she seemed very happy. Life would go on as before.

The couple of hours they talked together went all too quickly, and

Colin made a move to leave as he'd told Ella and his children that he would be in the gardens when they returned. They gave each other a hug and a kiss on the cheek and moved on for a second time. They both felt a little sad about having to part again, but each was satisfied knowing the other was well cared for and loved. Even though feelings can hurt for a while, sometimes life has a strange way of keeping those that are right in your life on the right track, and there can never be any harm in caring for someone.

Colin met Ella and the children, who were all excited about their sail and could not wait to tell him all about it. He listened and asked questions and found that they were very happy with their afternoon's fun. Ella asked what he had done to pass the time. He told her he would tell her about it later, slipped his arm around her, and they walked to the nearest restaurant for dinner.

Conor and Emma were very hungry after their afternoon's activity, and giving them a good meal was the most important thing on Colin's mind. They were just one more happy family on vacation.

Ann returned to her apartment, prepared a meal, and sat in front of the television to eat it. Before she started to eat, she pulled her phone out of her purse to check for messages. There was a message from Shane. It said he would call her later that evening. She was anxious to hear from him and kept herself busy while waiting for his call.

He did call later in the evening and told her he was almost finished with his work there and would be back home within the week. Ann had only a couple days left in her course and she would be home on the weekend. It would be so nice to be together again.

On her last Friday afternoon, Ann was glad to close out her apartment, gather up her belongings, and head for her home in Guysborough. She texted Shane and let him know she was back home. She had just put the kettle on to make a cup of tea when the doorbell rang. She wondered who it could be, since she had only come home a very short time ago. She turned the kettle off and went to the door.

"Surprise!" shouted Shane, as he picked her up and spun her around.

"Oh, this is great! When did you get here?"

"I got here about an hour ago. I am so happy to see you. I thought I wouldn't see you until tomorrow."

They walked arm in arm down the hall to the kitchen where Ann turned the kettle back on. The two of them made sandwiches, and with some cookies they found in the cupboard, they sat down to eat and talk. They had so much to catch up on. There was a wedding to plan, and they had to discuss it.

They ate and talked. The subject of their conversation was about their wedding. Where were they going to get married? Would they get married at Shane's home or Ann's home? Would they even get married at one of their homes? The discussion continued on with no solution in sight. They finally decided to leave it for the moment. Time would bring a solution to the issue.

"Let's do something else and leave the question alone for now.

We'll come up with an answer. There's probably a very simple one," declared Ann.

"Good idea." Shane changed the subject. "Do you have your violin with you?"

Ann nodded and walked to the piano, where the violin always rested. She picked it up and Shane struck the piano keys as she made sure it was in tune. They played all their favourite pieces, finishing off as usual with "The Old Violin," their favourite piece of music.

The hour was getting late and both of them were really tired, having put in long hours for the past month. They decided to call it a day and made an appointment to take their bicycles and meet, where the two driveways connected, at nine o'clock on Saturday morning. They kissed goodnight, and Shane left for his house. Within the half hour, Ann was in bed and fast asleep.

Chapter 18

A Wish Come True

MORNING CAME ALL TOO quickly for Ann, as she could have stayed in bed for another hour or so but had promised to meet Shane at nine o'clock. She bounded out of bed, took a quick shower, dressed, and was out the door in a flash. Shane was waiting for her when she arrived. They chatted for a few minutes and then were off down the hill to their spot on the sand. It was a beautiful, warm, sunny day, with a slight breeze. They sat there for some time, and as usual, topics of conversation were not scarce. There main topic now was their wedding, and the main subject was where it would be held. They talked about it for some time with several places being mentioned.

Evidently it was something that was not going to be settled on immediately. Time was passing, so they decided to ride their bikes to the restaurant in Guysborough for some breakfast.

Riding their bicycles was always a pleasure for each of them, and the day was just perfect for their endeavour. They entered the restaurant and took a seat by the window. There were not too many people there. However, they did notice two young gentlemen they had seen there before. They were sitting at the table next to Ann and Shane, speaking good English but with accents. Ann and Shane ordered, and again started talking about the place they would like to hold their wedding.

"Tell me, Ann," asked Shane, "have you ever dreamed of a place where you would love to be married? Maybe you'd like to get married down by the river. Tell me, because whatever you want, I will certainly go along with it."

Ann shifted on her chair. She was deep in thought for a few seconds. Then said, "Yes, there is a place I would love to have as a backdrop for our wedding. I'm afraid you'll laugh at me, but I always dreamed of a waterfall. I think it would make a great place for a wedding ceremony. It would make a terrific backdrop, and the pictures would be different and lovely."

Shane thought about that for a minute or two, then he picked up Ann's hand and looked at her. "If that's what you want, I'll be happy with that. But I don't know of any waterfalls in this area."

The two gentlemen sitting at the table next to them were evidently overhearing their conversation.

"Excuse us," said one of the gentlemen, after looking at his table mate, "we could not help but hear your conversation. If you wish, we can tell you where there is a waterfall in the area, and it is not too very far from here. First, please allow us to introduce ourselves. I am Josef

Fischer, and this is my brother Bruno. We are from Germany. We have a home here in the area, and we spend quite a bit of time around here, especially during the summer. We hope you will excuse us if you feel we are intruding."

Shane got to his feet. "Hello, it's so nice to meet you. We've seen you in here before. I'm Shane Robertson and this is my fiancée, Ann Blair. You're not intruding at all. We'd love help in finding a waterfall nearby."

"We do know of one. It's on a privately owned property on the North Riverside Road."

"That's very close to our homes!" Ann said.

"We know the owner quite well," Josef said. "He is a very amicable gentleman. We cannot speak for him, but we are sure he will be glad to listen to your request. He has a home on this beautiful property and keeps it immaculate, so we are sure that, if he agrees to let you use it, there will be some stipulations you will have to follow. His name is Jake Sheridan. You cannot see his property from the road, but if you go to the other side of the river, it is in plain view. If you wish, you should go and have a talk with him. He is fairly direct, so I am sure he will give you his answer right away."

"Thank you so much," said Shane. "We appreciate your information. Would you like to join us? We have seen you and your brother here many times. Maybe it's time we became acquainted."

"Why thank you," answered Josef. "We would like that."

The four of them sat, ate, and talked for some time. They all seemed very pleased to meet new friends. In the space of time they were there, they gained much information about each other. Ann and Shane found out that the German brothers were from the city of Bremen, located in northwestern Germany. Bremen is the tenth most populous city in Germany and noted for its fine wines. It has the world's largest wine cellar, which is located beneath the main square of Bremen. The two brothers ran a business there and were currently on vacation.

Bruno and Josef found out that Shane was a writer and also a very good pianist. He had written many books and had some of them on the bestsellers list. They were surprised when they found out that Ann was a senior mathematics teacher, a job that was usually held by men in Germany. On learning that Ann was an accomplished violinist, they expressed a desire to hear her play.

"The next time we get together with our families, we'll invite you to come and join us. We're sure both our parents, and also Ann's grandmother, would love to meet you," declared Shane as he stood up. It was time he and Ann returned home.

The Fischer brothers rose as well and said that they also had to be on their way.

"It was so nice to finally meet you," said Bruno. "We saw you in here so many times and felt you must be from the area. Goodbye for now, and we will keep in touch. Let us know how you make out with Jake Sheridan. We are sure you will like him."

They shook hands, and the Fischer brothers departed. Ann and Shane paid their bill and left for home. On the way back, they discussed visiting Jake Sheridan, thinking that perhaps they had better give him a call first, and that there was no better time than right now.

They rode their bicycles back to Ann's house, and upon entering the house, Ann immediately grabbed the phone book and hunted up Jake Sheridan's name. She found it and let Shane make the call.

Jake Sheridan answered the call immediately. Shane explained who he was and told him how he happened to hear about him and his property. He then told him that he and Ann were getting married in June and that Ann had expressed a desire to be married by a waterfall.

"The Fischer brothers heard us wondering about whether there was a waterfall in the area, and they mentioned your property. Could we make an appointment to come and talk with you or is the answer no right away?"

Jake was a little surprised by the request, but he told Shane that he would certainly like to meet them and would talk with them. They made an appointment for the next day. Shane was delighted. Even if he didn't want to allow them on his property, he sounded like a very nice person, and after all, he was a neighbour. It would be nice to get to know him.

The next day dawned a bit cloudy and warm. Shane drove up for Ann and they set off to visit Jake Sheridan. As they drove up his driveway, they realized the image they had seen of the place from across the river in no way measured up to what they saw as they made their way up the driveway. The owner was busy hanging up a hummingbird feeder.

Seeing them, he climbed down from a small stool and came to

meet his guests. He was an average-sized man with a big smile and a hand extended to make their acquaintance. Ann and Shane liked him immediately.

"You have a beautiful place here," exclaimed Shane.

"Thank you," said Jake.

They spent a few minutes chatting and then Jake said, "I understand you two are getting married and would like to be married beside a waterfall. Come, I will show you the nearest one on my property. It's not too far from the house and has a nice flow of water over it right now."

He led them down a well-trodden path to the falls below the house. There had been a rainfall the night before, and the falls were in full bloom with water gushing down and spilling into a stream below. It was almost at its best.

Ann just stood there completely in awe at the sight before her.

"Oh, that is so beautiful!" Ann exclaimed. "That is exactly what I envisioned. You are so lucky to have such a spectacle on your property."

"It is so beautiful," Shane said. "Nature at its best."

Jake was pleased that they seemed to be enjoying these falls as much as he and his family did. One of the last things he did every evening, when the weather permitted, was to walk down to these falls and stand for a few minutes to enjoy the flow of water over the rocks and peacefully glide away in the stream below. To him there was no better way to end his day. His problems just seemed to disappear down the runnel, and his mind cleared as the water drifted on to its destination.

Ann turned and looked at Mr. Sheridan.

"Could I ask you a question, sir?" she nervously said.

"Yes, certainly, ask away," answered Jake.

"I would love to be married beside a waterfall. This is perfect. Would you consider allowing us to be married here beside this one?"

"Yes, I'd be honoured to have a marriage take place here. There are a few things we would have to consider of course. Let's go up to the house, and we can discuss it over a cup of coffee."

They followed Jake back up the trail to the large edifice at the top of the hill and made their way inside, after they stopped to pet the two friendly dogs lying at the large entrance to the house. Jake ushered them into the kitchen and plugged in the electric kettle. Ann and Shane pulled out two chairs at the kitchen table and sat down. Jake did the same as they waited for the kettle to boil.

"When is the wedding?" asked Jake.

"Next June, on the thirtieth of the month," Shane said, "as Ann is a teacher and works until almost the end of the month."

"That sounds fine. The weather will be fine then, at least as much as one can depend on the weather. However, there are a few things I must ask that you do. How many guests will there be?"

Shane looked at Ann and they both thought for a minute.

"Probably no more than seventy," replied Ann.

"That will mean quite a number of vehicles. As you can see, there's not much room for parking here on the hill. I would have to ask that parking take place down below and the guests be transported up the hill. There's a great place to park cars down the road a short distance.

Folks can leave their cars there and be driven up the driveway. That way, there will be no parking problem. Could you manage that, or maybe I could handle that for you?"

"We would have no problem with that. It sounds great, and no one would have any trouble finding a place to park," responded Shane, with a big smile on his face.

"Does this mean you'll consider letting us get married at your waterfalls?" Ann blurted out excitedly.

"Yes, I will. Will some of the pictures be taken here and where will the reception be?" returned Jake.

Ann looked at Shane and then told Jake final plans had not been made as of yet, but they thought the reception would be at her house and the party afterwards at Shane's house. The two houses were partially on the same driveway and transportation to Shane's house could be handled the same way as it would be looked after at Jake's place. That way there would be less confusion. As for the pictures, some of them would be taken at the falls, since it was so beautiful there.

"That will be fine. I just want to know so I can have things ready for you," replied Jake.

"We'll pay you for the inconvenience," ventured Shane. "We can't expect you to go to extra work for us. You did not even know we existed until a few hours ago."

Jake shook his head. "I don't want any money for it. I didn't know you personally, but I did know you existed. I've seen you around the area a few times at the restaurant and on your bicycles. It's so nice to finally meet you. I'd love to meet your parents some time as well."

"The next time we have a family dinner, you'll be invited. We're sure you'll like our parents, and they would like to meet you as well," said Ann.

Shane spoke up and thanked Jake for allowing them to have their wish of a waterfall for their wedding.

"We have to go now. It's so nice to meet you and thank you again for granting us our wish. We'll keep in touch."

Shane and Jake shook hands, and he and Ann waved to Jake as they drove out the driveway.

"We just met a really nice neighbour," declared Ann.

Ann and Shane were very pleased with their morning's work. They now had the place for the wedding ceremony, the reception, and the following festivities. They would talk these over with their mothers and leave the rest of the planning to them. It seemed they were anxious to get started on that part of the wedding, and both Ann and Shane were glad to have them handle it.

Ann and Shane noticed when they came out of Jake's house that the wind had come up and there was quite a stiff breeze blowing. It was starting to look like a storm was coming in. As they made their way out of the driveway, they noticed the water on the river was very choppy.

"Oh, look," exclaimed Ann. "There's a small boat out on the river, and there are two people in it. They look as though they're having trouble. We had better see if we can help them!"

Shane stopped the car at the bottom of Jake's driveway and ran out onto the beach. One of the occupants of the boat was waving to him. They looked desperate and needed help. He handed his phone to Ann.

"Call Mr. Sheridan! Tell him the problem. Ask him if he'll help us. I'll swim out to the boat. It looks as though it may be two children!"

Ann made the call, and Jake said he would be right there. She placed Shane's phone down on her hat on the beach and started to swim out to the boat behind Shane, who reached the boat shortly before her. Just as she reached the boat, a huge wave caught it and hurled it toward her. She did not have time to get out of the way, and it hit her on the head and knocked her out.

Shane heard a loud thump and then saw the blood gushing from a large gash in her head. He almost panicked but then swung into action. He told the two children to sit down and hold on as tight as they could. He would have to tend to Ann first. Just then, Jake appeared on the scene. At first, he wasn't fully aware of the situation. Then Shane hollered to him.

"Jake, can you swim?"

"Yes, I can," hollered Jake.

"Come quick! Ann is hurt! I need help!"

Jake swam out to where Shane and Ann were. He immediately saw the seriousness of the situation.

Shane asked Jake if he would tend to the two kids while he got Ann back to shore. Ann was going in and out of consciousness, and her head was bleeding. He managed to grab her and hold her head above water while he half floated, half carried her to shore.

Once back on land, he saw where Ann had left his phone and called 911. He stayed with her, took off his shirt, and wrapped it around her head. It was still bleeding steadily but not as much as at the beginning. He then turned his attention to Jake and the two children in the boat. Jake was struggling to get the them to sit down. It was plain to see that they were terrified.

It was only a small boat, so he tried to see if he could pull it to shore, but that was not to be. The wind was too strong, and the waves turned the boat in all directions. The children had lost the oars minutes before they had called out to Ann and Shane on shore, as the boat heaved about in the rough water.

Shane stood up and hollered to Jake.

"Ask the kids if they can swim! If they can, you may be able to bring them to shore one at a time."

Jake found out that the children could not swim, and they did not have lifejackets. *Good grief*, he thought. *Do their parents know they're out here?* He decided he could not take one ashore and leave the other. The one that was left might panic and drown. He would just have to hold the boat and keep them as calm as he could until Shane, or someone else who happened by, could come to help him.

It was almost twenty-five minutes before the ambulance came to get Ann. Shane went with Ann to the hospital in Guysborough, and one of the ambulance attendants stayed, swimming out to help Jake with the two children. The wind was getting stronger. It was raining now, and there were flashes of lightning and loud claps of thunder.

The two children were beyond terrified by this time. The temperature had turned colder, and they were shivering and very wet. When the ambulance attendant arrived, he grabbed one of the children and Jake took the other one. The two kids were so afraid that they had a difficult time getting them out of the boat.

Finally, both men managed to pry them loose and began to swim with them to shore. It was hard going with a petrified child clinging to each of them. Both men managed to get the two young people back to shore but were totally exhausted when they got there. The young kids were terrified and crying. They started to shiver, and Jake insisted they both get into his truck, and he would take them up to his house to warm them up and get some particulars on them. The four of them huddled into Jake's truck, and he drove back up his driveway.

The weather had turned really miserable. It was now windy and raining with thunder and lightning. Jake's dogs were running around. They dreaded thunder. They paced the floor and were ready to hop up on the knee of anyone who would accept them.

Jake's wet visitors were trembling in their wet clothes. He found some warm blankets and told them to take their wet clothes off and wrap themselves in the blankets. He would throw their wet clothes in the dryer. After completing that, he made all of them hot chocolate and produced some cookies. The two youngsters were still trembling from their episode in the water and were only too glad to partake of his generosity.

After things started to quiet down and the trembling stopped, Jake set about trying to find out who the two young people were. They told him their names were Tommy and Marilyn MacDonald. Jake had heard of the MacDonalds, who lived across the river from him, but he had never met them. Tommy told Jake their phone number, and he called to tell the parents that the children were fine and that, if they could not come for them, he would take them home. He told the parents it was a long story, and he would let Tommy and Marilyn report the happenings themselves.

Finally, the dryer dinged, letting them know the clothes were dry. The three of them got back into their own clothes, and with that and the hot chocolate and cookies, they seemed to be in better cheer and no longer trembling. The thunder had subsided by this time, and the dogs were no longer on the prowl. They had settled down and were looking at the two youngsters with the hope that they might go outside and throw the ball around for them.

This did not happen as the father of the youths arrived for them and was so very thankful to Jake and the ambulance attendant for rescuing them. It was difficult to say what might have happened to them if Ann and Shane had not seen them out on the water. Tommy and Marilyn gave Jake a hug, thanked him for saving them, drying their clothes, the hot chocolate, and cookies, gave the dogs a pat, and then they followed their father to the car.

As soon as they left, Jake drove the attendant to the hospital in Guysborough. By this time, Ann and Shane were already on their way to the hospital in Antigonish. She was fully conscious and the gash on her head had been tended to, but the doctor just felt she should do a couple of tests to be sure there would be no complications. Shane had called Ann's parents and his parents, and of course, each couple drove to the hospital immediately. On their arrival, they found Shane pacing the floor with worry. He didn't know if the parents would be a help or a hindrance. However, he felt they should know.

Shane sat with the two sets of parents in a small waiting room and told them what had happened. He said that the two children were still in the boat when he left, and one of the ambulance attendants and Jake Sheridan were tending to them. He hoped they managed to get them to shore safely as the weather had turned nasty after he left with Ann.

Finally, Ann's doctor in Antigonish came to see Shane and told him they were going to keep Ann overnight, just to be sure she was all right. He said they had done some tests, and it appeared to be just a bad bump on the head with a mean gash. She would have to take it easy for a week or so, but she should be fine.

Shane sat down, relieved. He'd been afraid she had been seriously injured. However, it was still a bump to the head, and he would see that she did what she was supposed to. Ann could be very careful when looking after someone else but not so heedful when it came to herself.

Shane and his parents went back to his place and Ann's parents went to Ann's place. They were all worried over Ann but glad the doctor said she had done the tests and felt she would be all right. It was still a worry. An injury of any kind was serious but one to the head was most certainly not to be ignored. Shane was determined to make sure Ann got the rest she needed.

Ann came home the following afternoon, and Bill and Barbara were determined they would make her lie low for a few days and keep careful watch over her to see that there were no signs of complications. Shane visited often. His parents had gone home, and he was back to his writing.

Ann did as she was told for a few days, but as she began to feel better, she was up and on the go again. It was getting close to the time school started for the coming term, so she started to think about lesson plans for her grade eleven and twelve classes.

Her head still hurt a little, but it was more from the gash in her scalp than the bump on her head. It had not healed completely yet and washing her hair and brushing and combing it was a problem. Some of the hair had to be shaved close to the cut, and she had to comb her hair over it to hide the scar. Her mother helped her with the comb over but the hair would not always stay in place. It was not good, but it could have been much worse. The smash on her head when the boat hit her could have caused a really big problem. As it was, there seemed to be no issues from it.

On her release from the hospital, Ann told her parents and Grammie, who was now with them, the whole story of what happened and how she had been hurt. She also told them about Jake Sheridan and how they came to meet him. They were pleased when she told them that Mr. Sheridan agreed to allow them to get married near the falls on his property.

It seemed like such a perfect setting. Barbara was really pleased, for now that the place for the wedding was settled, she and Elsie could start handling the other details, with Shane and Ann's approval of course.

There would be time for planning, but in the meantime, life must go on. Ann had to get back to her job, and Shane had a book to finish and another one to write before the big day. As each day passed, Ann's head was feeling much better. The gash was completely healed and her hair had started to grow back in. Although she would rather stay in Guysborough, she had to get back to her home and her job. She visited Shane to say goodbye and then left.

The school year started with the usual confusion of the first few days. Her classes were large with more than thirty students in each class. Everyday life carried on, and before she knew it, it was Thanksgiving weekend.

Chapter 19
Ann Remembers...

SATURDAY MORNING ARRIVED AND Ann drove to Guysborough. Her parents were already there. She took her suitcase up to her room and then called Shane to let him know she had arrived. He texted her right back telling her he would meet her in ten minutes at the divide in the driveway. Ann took a few minutes to freshen up, told Barbara where she was going, grabbed a sweater as it was a warm day, and headed out to meet Shane. He was waiting for her when she arrived at the designated spot.

They were delighted to see each other again, and kissed and held each other for a few minutes before jumping on their bikes and riding to their favourite spot on the beach.

As the day was really warm, they sat on the sand and talked and caught up on all the news of the past week. All of a sudden, Ann put her hand into the pocket of the sweater she was wearing and her hand touched a piece of paper. Surprised, she pulled it out and opened it.

"What is it, Ann?"

Ann was wearing the sweater she'd worn on the night she showed the family the piece of paper from the old violin case that showed the two families were related. That night, she'd felt they had enough to think about and decided she would show it to Shane when they were alone. With all that had happened in the meantime, she had completely forgotten about it. She handed the paper to Shane.

"What is this? Where did you get it?" Shane stared at the paper. "It's a map!"

"I found it in the old violin case the last time I searched it. I was going to show it to our families at the same time as the paper that showed we were related, but everyone was so shocked to find out the other news, I thought I would leave it for another time. I completely forgot about it. I guess too much has happened since then."

Shane studied the map on the piece of paper.

"It looks as though it would lead across the road from our driveway." He thought about that for a minute, and then said, "Did you have breakfast yet?"

She told him she hadn't, and they decided to visit the restaurant down the road. They rode their bicycles down and went in. They picked their usual table close to the window, and to their surprise, the two Fischer brothers were seated in their usual place. It looked as though they had not been served yet, so Shane asked them to join

Ann and him at their table. They obliged and the four of them ate and talked for over an hour.

Shane told them about their visit to Jake Sheridan and how pleased they were that he had agreed to allow them to be married at the falls on his property. He thanked the brothers for their information and assured them they would have an invitation to the wedding. They were a friendly foursome, and it was almost certain they would be good friends from then on.

Throughout the course of their conversation, Shane got the feeling the two brothers were familiar with most of the land in the area, having travelled on their snowmobiles during their winter visits and their all-terrain vehicles in the other seasons of the year. He looked at Ann as they talked, and she got the unspoken message. She produced the map she had found and inquired if they had ever been in the area close to their homes. They said they had during the winter but never in the other seasons, as the vegetation there was so thick.

Bruno asked Ann where she had found the map and she told him it was in her great-grandfather's old violin case. They were wondering if it meant there was something there or if it could be just a worthless piece of paper.

"There is only one way to find out," Josef said. "If you want some help with following the map, we would be glad to help you. We are very familiar with the countryside here as we do a lot of travelling in the woods."

Shane and Ann were pleased to hear them offer to help. They were not familiar with the wooded area around their houses and were likely to get lost if they ventured too far from home. It would certainly be nice to have some backup here. They decided to go home, don some clothes more appropriate for travelling in the forest, and meet back at the end of Ann and Shane's driveway in an hour.

Ann went home, changed into something more suitable for the mission she was on, told her mother where she was going, and left to meet Shane, Josef, and Bruno at the slated spot.

The Fischer brothers arrived with an axe and a small power saw. It was quite obvious they were used to going on such outings, and they came prepared, which was something Shane and Ann had not even thought of. Ann produced the map, and they went in search of the path that was mapped out on the paper.

The brush was very thick along the area where they figured the path should start. They searched for some time, and then Josef noticed a piece of lumber that was evidently used at some time to go across the ditch to get into the wooded area. Bruno cut the bushes around and on both sides of the piece of lumber. It became clear that there was definitely a well-trodden path there at one time.

It was still quite evident, even though grass covered it and huge ferns hindered anyone who might be in a hurry. The ferns were not deep rooted and could easily be removed. Once they got into the bushes, it was clear that a vehicle might have driven over it at one time. They continued on for some time, pulling ferns and cutting bushes that had grown over the path. The walked on for what seemed like a fair distance from where they had entered the wooded area, when all of a sudden, they stepped out of the woods and into what appeared to be a small field.

They stood there in amazement. Off to one side was the cabin they were searching for, and they all stopped and looked at it for a moment, before trudging over to it.

It was not very big, probably about twelve feet by twelve feet, and was painted grey with a metal roof. The door was black, and there were five windows, one on each side of the door and one on each of the other three sides. They walked up to try the door and found it was locked. They tried the windows, but they were firmly secured as well.

"There cannot be many people who know this is here or it would have been broken into long ago," Shane said.

They peered in through the windows. There was a stove, table, and two chairs in the one-room building. Another thing that caught Ann's eye was a music stand almost hidden behind the table. She pointed it out to Shane.

"Oh" declared Josef, "whoever this belonged to was definitely a musician! I don't think anyone else would have a music stand here."

"Yes," declared Ann. "I believe it belonged to my great-grandfather, although there is no mention of a second cabin on the deed to his land. I wonder why he would want a second cabin? The music stand makes me think he came here to play his violin and compose his music. I guess he liked to work alone."

They looked around for a while longer and then wended their way back out the path they came in on, pulling out more ferns as they travelled out. As Ann walked along, something began to come back to her. She remembered the first time she visited the cabin where her house now stood. She had stood and looked at her newly found inheritance, spying a key lying on a window sill.

She remembered picking it up and putting it in her jacket pocket. The question now was if she still had the jacket. She thought she likely did, as she hadn't thrown out any clothes lately. The jacket must be at home in her hall closet. If so, she could easily locate it. There was a possibility that it was the key that would open the small cabin they had just located. Ann came to the conclusion that this was a very interesting discovery.

They were soon back to their driveway, said goodbye to the Fischer brothers, and told them they would be in touch very soon. Shane said his feet were very wet so he had to go home to change. Ann agreed that she too was feeling a little soggy and wanted to go home to have a nice hot bath. She was cold and very damp. They kissed and then strolled up their separate driveways, agreeing to meet later in the evening.

It was decided earlier that they would have their Thanksgiving dinner on Sunday, as Ann had to leave early on Monday to prepare for school on Tuesday. The Blairs were having the dinner this time, and Barbara, Ann, and Grammie were very busy with the preparations. Ann told them all about their trip to the cabin the day before and how surprised they had been to find another small cabin back in the woods. She said that the Fischer brothers were a big help to them.

"Oh dear," she said. "I'll bet the two brothers are alone for Thanksgiving. I know it's not their Thanksgiving or if they have such a thing in their country, but I think it would be nice if we invited them to spend Thanksgiving dinner with us. Mom, do you mind if I invite them to eat with us?"

"No, not at all," answered Barbara. "That's what Thanksgiving is all about."

Ann looked up their number in the phone book and called them. They were home and delighted to be asked. They said that they would gladly attend. They asked the time for the meal and told Ann they were looking forward to it. Barbara and Grammie were especially pleased that they would be meeting some new people.

THE ROBERTSONS AND THE Fischer brothers all arrived at about the same time and were invited into the living room. Shane and Ann sprang into action and served drinks before the meal. Following that, they were all seated at the table for a turkey dinner with all the trimmings. The next hour or so was spent eating, talking, and just having a pleasant time, with both families were pleased to meet Josef and Bruno.

Following the meal, the ladies cleaned up and the men retired to the living room again and enjoyed some time getting acquainted. The remainder of the evening was enjoyed with Shane on the piano and Ann on the violin. With this evening began more friendships to be enjoyed by all of them.

The next morning, Ann was out of bed early. Within the hour she was on her way to meet Shane at the junction in their driveways. Shane was there when she arrived. The rode their bikes down to the beach and sat on rocks near the water. It was an unusually warm morning for almost the middle of October.

The eagles were flying overhead, and every once in a while, one would swoop down and pick up a fish for its meal. They sat there for some time talking about their previous evening and how glad they were that Josef and Bruno could be with them. There were plans for the wedding that had to be completed right away, and they made some decisions in that regard. As always, when they were together the time seemed to fly. They sped off down the road to their favourite restaurant for breakfast and found their German friends were already there.

They were invited to sit with them and again they obliged. Josef and Bruno told them how much they enjoyed their time with both families on the previous evening. Ann assured them that, whenever they were in Nova Scotia, there would definitely be more occasions like that.

They finished their meal and rode back to their driveway. Ann told Shane she would probably not be back to Guysborough until Christmas. He promised to visit her in Lawson's Brook every chance he got. They held each other for a few minutes, kissed, and parted.

On Thanksgiving afternoon, Ann went back to her house in Lawson's Brook, did her laundry, and sat down to prepare her lessons for the coming week. She completed her lesson plans, ate supper, took a long hot bath, and crawled into bed. As usual, she had no problem falling asleep.

The time between Thanksgiving and Christmas passed quickly. During that time, Ann had several visits from Shane, and during his visits, many wedding plans were discussed. With Shane and Ann's approval, their mothers were handling the caterers, the decorating, the music, and all the other details that make up a wedding. The guest list was approved by the bride and groom, after Jake, Josef, and Bruno were added. Things seemed to be falling into place.

Ann was eating supper one evening, when all of a sudden, she thought about their trip to the cabin they'd found, not too far from her home in Guysborough.

"Oh, the key!" she said out loud, just as if someone was in the room with her.

She jumped up from the table and made her way to the hall closet in search of the jacket she'd had on the day she picked up the key she'd found on the window sill of the original cabin. She made her way through the coats and jackets she had hanging there.

"Aha, there it is!" she uttered loudly again.

She took it out of the closet, put her hand in the pocket on the right-hand side, and there it was: a fairly large key. Surely it was the one that would open the door of the mysterious cabin they'd found. She went immediately to her purse and placed the key in a pocket with a zipper on it, so there would be no chance of losing it. The next time she was down in Guysborough, they would make a second trip to that little rustic cottage and discover what secrets she would find there.

Christmas came so quickly that Ann barely had time to do her shopping. She managed to get it done between school and housework, and on the last day of school before the holidays, she packed a few things (along with her Christmas gifts) and left for Guysborough.

Her parents were already there, and the smell of holiday baking was in the air as she opened the door. She carried her belongings in and put her gifts under the tree, which her parents already had up and decorated. The house was very festive, since her mother was quite gifted at decorating and making a place feel warm, comfortable, and in season. She took her suitcase up to her bedroom, along with Shane's gift. She would give it to him when they were alone.

Ann set the table for supper, and just as they were about to sit down, Shane arrived. He was immediately invited to sit with them, and as always, a pleasant meal was enjoyed and the conversation was amiable and jovial.

Chapter 20

A Big Surprise

TIME WAS PASSING, AND it was just two days before Christmas Day. The morning was crisp and bright as Ann got out of bed and prepared for the day ahead. There was only a wisp of snow on the ground, and she and Shane planned to go back to the cabin in the woods to see if the key she had would open the door.

The Fischer brothers were in Canada with their whole family for Christmas, but they were very busy that day, which meant she and Shane would have to make the trip on their own. Ordinarily Ann's father would have gone with them, but he and Barbara were on their way to Antigonish for their last shopping before Christmas. They were destined to make the trip on their own.

Ann met Shane at the end of their driveways, and they were off to visit the cabin in the woods. The walk in was fine, and they made it in what seemed like much less time than it had taken the first time they'd made their way into what had been unknown territory. As they approached the forsaken little cabin, Ann could not help but feel that it looked lonesome and alone and had been that way for quite some time. She wondered who had built it, and if it had actually been her great-grandfather, and why. If the key she carried opened the door, then perhaps they would get some answers.

They carefully made their way to the door, as there was more snow in the woods than in the open, and beneath the snow there were many branches and leaves that could trip them up if they were not careful. Ann produced the key. Shane took it, placed it in the lock, and "click," the door opened.

"Oh wow!" exclaimed Shane. "That was easy."

They entered the cabin and surveyed the contents. There was nothing there, other than what they had viewed through the window on their first visit. They took a second look.

"Wait a minute," Ann blurted out. "I wonder what's in that box under the table?"

There was a metal box about a foot square shoved under the table as far as it could go. Shane reached in and pulled it out. He lifted the cover. It was full of papers. At first glance, it appeared to be just plain, white paper. Then Ann picked a sheet of it up and turned it over. There was music written on the other side.

At the top of the page was what appeared to be the title of the hand written music. Ann turned the stack of papers over and found there was a piece of music written on every page, and each page had a title.

There were dozens of sheets, all with handwritten music on them and each with a name.

Ann looked at Shane. She was completely shocked. They both were completely stunned. They sifted through the tunes. Since they were both musicians, they knew these pieces of music were good.

Ann removed the music, and at the bottom of the box was a small notebook with the name "Alex Blair" in the cover. So that was settled. This was her great-grandfather's cabin. But why had he needed another cabin? He already had one.

She opened the notebook and began to read. It was a diary of the days he spent here, apparently writing music. He worked here because it was quiet and peaceful. No one bothered him here, and it was necessary to have alone time to concentrate and write his beloved music.

Well, thought Ann, *he certainly made use of the time. There are dozens of pieces of music here. They should have been published.*

She placed everything back in the box and snapped the lid back on. "This is coming with us," she said and handed the box to Shane.

"I'll take that music stand with me," she said. "These are definitely keepsakes, and I'll keep them always. This is family history. Dad and Grannie will be so interested in these."

Ann and Shane stood and looked around the cabin again, then walked out the door, and Shane locked it back up. This cabin was on Ann's land, and she decided it would stay as it was unless something unforeseen happened.

They walked back from the cabin, with Shane carrying the box full of music and Ann the music stand. Ann wished the articles they toted could talk. They would likely have quite a story to tell.

When they arrived back at Ann's house, the only one home was Grammie. As they told her their discovery, she was completely mesmerized at what they had found. Alex Blair had been a very secretive man and rarely disclosed what he did with his time, so this was just another of his reticent acts.

Ann made Shane and Grammie some lunch, and then she and Shane went about sorting out the music they had found and playing the pieces one by one. Grammie was thoroughly entertained. Some of the tunes were beautiful, and none of them had ever been played in public. They spent the afternoon and well into the evening going through the box of music and played each piece over several times.

"These are beautiful pieces of music," Shane declared. "We have to do something with them. They can't just lie here in a box. They are so good. They should be published."

"The only way that will happen is if you and I do it," declared Ann.

"I agree with the both of you," interrupted Grammie, "and the only people who can get them published are you two. So, you had better get to work. Alex would be so proud to have some of his creations published. It will take some work and a great amount of time though."

Ann set the music aside and went back to the box for the diary Alex had kept. As she read through it, she found that he had written a little story on each piece that he had created. Apparently, many of his musical compositions came to him as he sat in the cabin and just watched nature happen around him. The names on many of the tunes indicated that: "The Robin in the Tree;" "The Red Squirrel;" "Drifting Snow;" "The Mighty North Wind;" "The Swaying Trees;" and "Diamonds on the Snow" were only a few of the many pieces of music contained in the box, and there was a story attached to each one. Ann looked at Shane for a few seconds.

"I believe we have something here," she told him.

Shane agreed. "We could print the music and attach the story he has written to each corresponding melody. This could make a great book of music. It would be a terrific book for someone learning to play, as none of the pieces are extremely difficult. We can do this, Ann. I am always writing, so I know all about how to get it published and printed. I am sure the ones who do my other books would gladly print it for us."

Now, the two of them were on a mission. Not only did they have a wedding coming up but they were also publishing a book of music. However, Christmas was almost here, and they decided to put it aside for a couple of days and just enjoy the season. After all, it only came once a year.

The Robertsons were hosting the Christmas dinner this year, and the Christmas Eve festivities were up to the Blairs, who were determined to invite some new guests. Their list included Bruno and Josef and their girlfriends, along with Erich and Hannah, the Fischer brothers' parents and Jake Sheridan.

They spent all of Christmas evening having a few drinks, some holiday food, telling stories, and listening to Shane and Ann play. This time they played some of the new tunes they had just discovered. Bruno and Josef were especially interested in hearing about their return trip to the cabin. They asked where Ann had found the key and she related the story to them. Josef said he would like to make a return trip to the cabin one day soon, as he'd never been inside.

The evening passed all too quickly, and as the time was well past midnight and Christmas day was already here, everyone decided to get a little sleep. The Fischers', along with Elsie and John Robertson, left for home while Bill, Barbara, and Grammie headed for bed. Shane and Ann were finally left alone.

Ann excused herself for a minute and ran upstairs, returning with a beautifully wrapped gift. She kissed Shane, wished him a Merry Christmas, and handed it to him. He kissed her and took the gift.

"Thank you! Do you want me to open it now?"

"Oh, yes, I do. After all, it's Christmas now. Open it. Open it!" she said as she sat down next to him on the sofa.

Shane carefully untied the ribbon, loosened the tapes holding it together, and uncovered a beautiful box covered in red leather. He opened it and let out a gasp.

"Wow! This is beautiful!" exclaimed Shane.

He removed a gold pocket watch, with its inside cover engraved with his name and Ann's, along with the date. Inside the box, there were also two gold cuff links with his initials on them, and a gold tie tack, also with his initials.

"Ann, this is something I always wanted. So often I have to attend a wedding or a special occasion and just had cheap cuff links and a tie tack that didn't match. And I never ever had a pocket watch. I always thought they looked so sharp. Thank you! I love you so much. You know me. I think you can read my mind. Thank you! Thank you! I love it."

They talked for a few more minutes, and then Shane said he had better leave if he didn't want to fall asleep at dinner later on. He gave her a hug and told her he would be back soon. Ann locked the door behind him and went up to bed. She was especially happy that Shane loved his gift from her.

Ann awoke to the sound of the other members of the family talking, and it seemed they were opening gifts. She jumped out of bed, grabbed her robe, and bounded down the stairs. Her parents and Grammie were busy undoing their gifts, and hers were in a pile off to the side of the tree. She opened gifts along with the others and soon became aware that there was nothing there from Shane. Well, she would just have to wait a little longer.

Like every Christmas day, it passed by very quickly and soon the Fischer family and the Robertson family were all together again. Shane motioned to Ann. She grabbed her coat, and the two of them disappeared outside. They got into Shane's car and drove out the Blair's driveway and up the Robertsons'.

"Come on in with me," Shane told her.

They went into the house. They removed their coats, and Shane took her hand and led her to their Christmas tree. The other gifts had apparently been unwrapped. There was only one left. Shane picked it up and handed it to Ann.

"This is for you," he said. "I hope you like it."

Ann sat down, and Shane sat next to her. She unwrapped the package. Inside was a beautiful box, which coincidently, was also covered in red leather. She opened the lid and let out a gasp.

"Oh! Oh! Oh! It is beautiful! Oh, Shane, this is just so gorgeous. I love it, and I love you!"

Inside the box was a beautiful yellow-gold necklace covered with diamonds, and two earrings to match. Ann could not believe her eyes. She had never in her wildest dreams expected anything like that. It almost took her breath away.

Shane reached into the case, removed the necklace, and fastened it around Ann's neck. Then he removed the earrings, one at a time, and handed them to Ann as she placed them in her earlobes. She ran to the mirror in the hall to have a look at her finery. They were so beautiful, it brought tears to her eyes.

"They are so gorgeous!" she said with a shaking voice.

"Not nearly as beautiful as you," answered Shane as he put his arms around her and kissed her.

"I want to put them back in the box so the others can see them as I first did."

Shane unclasped the necklace for her, and she placed it back in the box along with the earrings. As she went to close the box, she noticed the inscription on the inside of the cover.

The inscription read, "To Ann, with all my love, from Shane" and the date.

Ann looked at the gift again before she closed the cover.

"I don't deserve such a beautiful gift. I can't thank you enough," she uttered.

Shane looked at her for a second. "Just seeing the look in your eyes when you opened it is all the thanks I will ever need. Wear it with pride, my dear Ann," he said, with tears in his eyes.

They returned to the Blair house, and Ann proudly revealed her gift from Shane. There were many "oohs" and "woos" as each one viewed it. Grammie told her she had better buy a safe and get it insured.

Later they all sat down to a delicious Christmas dinner with all the trimmings. The conversation was light, and the sound of laughter prevailed. Good friends can make good conversation, and that was certainly the order of the day.

Following the meal, Grammie and the men retired to the living room and the ladies cleaned up. It had been a busy time for them, and they were glad to join the others and just relax. As usual, Ann and Shane were asked to play for them, and they obliged. Again, they played some of the new music written by Alex Blair, and it was enjoyed by all. They ended with playing their favourite piece of all: "The Old Violin" also written by Alex Blair. Everyone loved that piece of music, and it was the perfect ending to a perfect day.

The time passed all too quickly and soon it was past midnight. The Fischer and the Robertson families left for home and Grammie,

Barbara, and Bill went off to bed. Shane and Ann were left alone. They sat and talked for a few minutes.

Ann thanked Shane again for the beautiful gift and told him she would treasure it forever. Shane told her he was very happy with the gift she had given him too, and he would certainly wear it on their wedding day. They kissed goodnight, and Shane left, telling her he would be back the next day, and they would get a start on the book they planned to do with the music they had found written by Alex Blair. Ann went off to bed feeling it was the best Christmas day ever.

The following day, Ann and Shane went to work on the music book they planned to produce. They sorted the music from the easiest piece to the most difficult. This meant playing each piece again, and sometimes several times if they could not decide which one should come ahead of the other.

Grammie situated herself where she was front and centre so she could enjoy each piece. It took them the whole week between Christmas and New Year's to organize the music, and then they had to read through Alex's diary and place the story he had written beside the appropriate piece of music. Copying the music and then typing the item to go with it was time consuming. Sometimes they could find a picture to go with the item, which added to the contents of the book but did take more time.

Things were progressing quite nicely when all at once they came across a complete surprise. They uncovered a piece of music not written by Alex Blair. Neither one of them had ever seen the music or heard it played before. It was titled "Hector the Hero."

"Wow!" shouted Ann. "This looks like it is a really good tune. Let's try it!"

Shane placed the piece of music up on the piano where Ann could see it, and she tried it. It took her a few tries before she got the right lilt to it. Shane listened and then started to accompany her. The accompaniment made it easier for her, and soon they were playing it quite well.

Grammie sat up in her chair and clapped.

"I know that piece!" she said. "Your great-grandfather played it many times. I love it. Play it again!"

They played it over and over, and each time, it was better. They loved it. It was comparable to "The Old Violin."

"Oh, this is great. Now we have two pieces of music people will love to hear played over and over again. We will have to do a little research to find out who wrote it and some information on the writer. What a great piece of music. I can't imagine why we never heard it before," Ann said. "Oh my, look at the time. We'll have to stop for now. Let's play that tune once more. Maybe we can play it tonight."

They played it over a few more times and then had to shut down operations for the New Year festivities.

The same group of people who were present for Christmas were also invited to the Robertsons' for New Year's celebrations, this time including Jake Sheridan. The Fischer family was thoroughly enjoying the celebrations as they were just a bit different from those in their home country. Ann and Shane played for them, and "Hector the Hero" was the hit they knew it would be.

Closure

THE FIRST OF JANUARY came and everyone was back to their usual jobs and homes. Time flew by and February was upon Ann before she knew what happened. Shane visited her during one weekend in January, which gave her a little break during the month. It was a fairly good winter as far as the weather was concerned. There was only one day when school was cancelled due to a snowstorm.

Whenever Ann had time, she worked on the book of Alex Blair's music. As March break approached, she had it all laid out, and with the exception of the first few pages and the closing, it was almost complete. She needed Shane's help and expertise to complete it for printing. She already had Grammie do a write up on Alex Blair, and she also came up with a good picture of him. Shane was the writer, so it was up to him to come up with the preface and ending, and to get the publishing and printing done.

On one weekend in February, Ann and her mother made a trip to

Halifax for her wedding dress. They had a great time and Ann found the wedding dress of her dreams. She managed to complete the entire attire for her big day, and there was another big checkmark on her list of things to do. Barbara and Elsie seemed to have everything else under control, and things were progressing nicely.

Shane was busy with his writing, taking time out on some weekends to spend time with Ann. The weather for most of the winter was fairly good for travelling, which was a good thing as he looked forward to his time with her and it gave him a couple of days to clear his head. To a person who did not write, or who had never written, it might seem like an easy job, but it took a great amount of thought, and sometimes, depending on the setting for your story, it also took a great amount of research.

At the present time, Shane was writing a novel with the main part of the story taking place in Northern Quebec. In April, he was going to take a trip there to make sure his descriptions for the area were correct. He had to wait until then though, because at that time of year, he was most likely to get some late winter storms and some early spring melts. This would be a good time to see much of the bad weather and some of the better weather he needed for his novel.

The winter months passed quickly. Ann spent her March break at her home in Guysborough with Shane. He took the week off from his writing to rest for a spell and be with her. Plans for the wedding were progressing nicely. With Barbara and Elsie in charge of the coming occasion, that was a big job out of their hands. Every time anyone mentioned the big day and its planned activities, Ann became more excited and was finding it harder and harder to wait for that day.

In late April, Shane left for his trip to Northern Quebec. He went to a community called Kangirsuk, located on the north shore of the Payne River, thirteen kilometers inland from Ungava Bay. The village lies between a rocky cliff to the north and a large, rocky hill to the west. The numerous lakes and rivers of the area are well known for their arctic char and lake trout. The strong tides push up the Payne River and make it a great place for mussel harvesting as well. The Hudson Bay Company was founded there. The municipality of Kangirsuk was incorporated in 1981.

A good part of the novel Shane was writing about took place around this area. He settled himself into a one-room cabin. It contained a stove, table, two chairs, and a bed. There were no frills, but it was all Shane needed for as long as he would be there. He ate his meals at a small diner just down the road from his cabin. His main aim was to get the feel for the type of life these people lived. He spent his days travelling the area. The spring was sometimes rough, and the ice on the river was starting to get large cracks in it. It really was not safe to walk on.

Eider ducks inhabited the islands close to the village, and the women of the village collected the precious down of these birds to make the warm parkas that protect the residents from the biting, winter cold. Shane tried as many of the local activities as he could, to get the real feel of their type of life.

On occasion, Shane would go out walking by himself. He would travel around the area, paying close attention to where he was in fear that he would get lost. To him, things in the area within walking distance all looked much the same. On one occasion, he was walking along a stream. It was probably about one hundred metres wide. The ice had broken up in some parts and some of the ice was floating and being carried off by the stream.

All of a sudden, he saw a little girl standing on the shore, crying and calling out. It took him a minute or two to figure out what was happening. Then he saw her pointing to a moving cake of ice with a medium-sized reddish brown and white dog on it. Her dog was floating down the stream. Immediately, Shane's heart went out to the little girl and her beloved dog.

He sprang into action. He ran to the stream, picked up a long branch that was lying on the bank of the stream, and some rope, and jumped out onto an ice cake. He carefully picked his way from one cake to another, heading in the direction of the dog. It took him several minutes to reach the cake with the dog on it.

All of a sudden, it occurred to him that his was a strange dog. It might not appreciate a stranger grabbing it and pulling it off the ice cake. He leaped onto the same one as the dog, and to his relief, it seemed the dog was thankful for Shane's help. It slid over toward his rescuer, and Shane tied the rope around it like a harness.

His job now was to get the dog to go from ice cake to ice cake to get back to shore. This was not going to be an easy task. There was only one thing to do and that was to go for it. He used the pole to bring another ice cake as close as possible to the one he and the dog were on. Then he jumped on it and was really surprised when the dog followed and jumped as well.

The two continued to move slowly from cake to cake, and everything went fine until they were almost to the shore. The ice cakes were not as large there, or as close together. Shane managed to pull one fairly close. He held the dog tight and jumped onto it.

The dog panicked and braced his feet. Even on the ice, he gave Shane quite a jerk and they slipped off the cake of ice and into the cold water. Fortunately, the water was shallow there. He pulled the dog close, grabbed it in his arms, and waded to shore, where the dog jumped down and ran to the little girl.

She was still crying but now it was for the man who was out in this cold weather now with dripping-wet clothes. The little girl spoke broken English, but Shane managed to understand enough of what she said to know that she was going to get help. She and the dog ran off, and he stood there shivering in the cold. He knew he had to keep moving or he would surely freeze to death.

He started to walk back the way he had come, but only went a short distance when he realised he probably couldn't make it, as his clothes were frozen stiff and clinging to his body. He tried to keep moving, but it was almost impossible.

He stopped and stood for a few seconds, and then he slowly settled to the ground. He didn't know how long he was there before he heard the little girl and some grownups coming toward him. Then he stopped hearing or seeing anything at all.

Unconscious, he was gathered up quickly, put into a car, and taken to the nearest house. It was some time later before Shane began to come around enough to remember some of what had happened. What he didn't know was that he was the talk of the village as the man who risked his life to save the little girl's dog.

More familiar with the cold and risks of hypothermia, this was an act that no man in the village would have attempted. It was just too dangerous. To them, a dog was not worth risking your life over. Shane would never see things that way. There was not just a dog involved here. There was a little girl's beloved pet. He could not just stand there and let her pet disappear forever. He would find it difficult to live with himself if he had let that happen.

Shane was told that the little girl had run home and told her father the situation. He had picked up a couple of their neighbours in his truck and raced to the shore, where they'd found Shane on the ground. They'd carried him to the truck and raced back to the father's home to warm him up.

He learned of all this while bundled up in the home of Jean Laduc, his wife Teresa, and Amy, the little girl whose dog he had rescued. The men had removed Shane's wet frozen clothes and wrapped some blankets around him, which Teresa had made nice and warm beforehand by placing them in the oven for a few minutes while awaiting their return.

Shane had come back to awareness lying on a couch near a stove.

He looked down, and lying on the floor beside his makeshift bed was the dog he'd rescued. The little girl was on the floor beside the dog. Amy looked worried but seemed a bit relieved when she saw Shane move. She'd run to tell her mother that the "man was awake."

The next thing Shane had noticed were his clothes stretched out around the stove. Obviously, they were trying to dry them for him. They were all heavy clothes to stave off the cold weather, so the drying process was going to take some time. Shane was shivering, so Teresa piled more blankets on him and then handed him a cup of hot tea.

He tried to sit up to drink it. With the weight of the blankets on him, it was not easy, but he managed to get the hot tea down, and it hit the spot. For a while, he could not stop shivering and then suddenly felt extremely hot and was throwing the blankets off. This back and forth of shivering and sweating went on for the remainder of the day and on into the night, as the Laducs felt he was too sick to go back to his cabin by himself, especially while his clothes remained damp.

He remained on the couch close to the stove, and even though the family went to bed much later in the evening, the dog remained beside him. Shane spent a very restless night, too hot one minute and freezing the next.

Jean Laduc was the first one up the next morning, and the first thing he did was check on Shane. Then he stoked the fires. He studied Shane for a moment. He didn't look well. There was a doctor in the village, and Jean called the man's house. It was early in the day, but the doctors in these villages were used to early calls.

Within the hour, Dr. Fillier was at the door. He took one look at Shane and knew he had a very sick man on his hands. Within a few minutes, he discovered that Shane's chest was congested, and he had an extremely high temperature.

The doctor gave Jean Laduc a prescription to have filled for Shane and said he would be back to check on him later in the day. Jean got the prescription filled as soon as the drugstore opened, and immediately after he arrived back home, he gave Shane his first dose.

Shane was very restless and spent most of the day falling in and out of sleep. He had developed a very harsh, dry cough and seemed to be in pain each time he coughed. Jean was sure his temperature had not decreased any, because his face was quite red and he was still shivering at times.

Dr. Fillier came back to see Shane early that evening and was not pleased with Shane's condition. He told Jean to keep giving him his medicine regularly and to make sure he drank plenty of fluids. If he was no better in the morning, he would have to be taken to the hospital. The doctor said he would be back first thing in the morning.

Jean did not go to bed that night. He slept on a recliner near the stove, where he would be sure to keep the stove stoked and give Shane his medicine on time. Getting Shane to drink was not a problem. He drank glass after glass of various fluids.

Shane put in another restless night and only dozed off for any real length of time around daybreak. It was obvious that he was not any better.

Amy's dog, whom the family simply called "Dog," put in the night for the second time lying on the mat beside Shane's couch. It was almost as though the dog knew Shane was sick because he had saved its life.

Jean immediately called Dr. Fillier and reported on Shane. He asked the doctor if he could come and see Shane as soon as possible. Dr. Fillier was there within the hour, examined Shane, and thought that, if anything, the man was getting worse. He made a couple of phone calls and told Jean he was having Shane moved to the Ungava Tulattavik Health Centre, which was located in Kuujjuaq and served seven villages along Ungava Bay Coast, Kangirsuk being one of them.

Shane was transported there by ambulance within the hour. He was tended to immediately, and given many tests and all the attention possible within the facility. He was so sick he hardly realized that he had moved from the Laduc's residence to the hospital. Nurses attended him around the clock and reported any changes to the attending doctor. Finally, on the third day after his admittance, he seemed to be a little brighter and was more attentive to what was happening around him.

Dr. Fillier visited him later on in the day and reported him as being a little better but not out of the woods yet. Shane had a severe case of pneumonia, and although he seemed to be on the road to recovery, he still had a long way to go. The doctor advised the nurses to keep him warm and comfortable and make sure he drank as much as possible.

Several days passed with Shane improving a little each day. He was sitting up more, and his appetite, (although not great) was much better. Things were coming back into reality for him. He knew he was very sick and in a hospital, but where and how he got there was now a bit of a mystery to him. He could only remember little bits of the time since rescuing the dog.

As he was lying in bed trying to recall the last few days, all of a sudden, it hit him. Looking to a nurse who had just entered the room, he said, "Could I ask you a question?"

"Why, certainly," she answered.

"I wonder where my phone, wallet, and clothes are."

"Your phone and wallet are in the safe here, and the clothes you had on when you fell into that icy water are in the closet here. Mr. Laduc brought in everything belonging to you."

Shane looked relieved and asked if it was possible for him to have his phone now. The nurse said she would get it for him but that it would be safer to leave his wallet in the safe. She left, and within a few minutes, she was back with his phone. It was dead, and he needed somewhere to recharge it.

He mentally thanked himself for splurging on its waterproof case, as it seemed no worse for wear, other than its dead battery. The nurse looked after the situation for him. She said that she would be back in a little while, and while the phone was charging, he should lie back down and go to sleep. She left, and within ten minutes, Shane did just that.

More than three hours later, Shane awoke with Dr. Fillier and the same nurse staring at him. The nurse placed a thermometer into his mouth and then took his blood pressure. The doctor examined the results and told Shane he would be taken shortly for a chest x-ray.

A few minutes later, an attendant arrived with a wheelchair. Shane was about to tell him he could walk, but as soon as he stood up, he knew that was not possible. He couldn't believe how weak he was. He was forced to settle for the wheelchair and was glad when the test was completed. The attendant wheeled Shane back to his bed and tucked him in. Shane was exhausted and immediately dosed off to sleep.

Later, the nurse returned with his phone, and Shane awoke with a start. He suddenly realized it was days since he'd had any connection with home and Ann. He knew they would be worried if they didn't hear from him. Even though there was a hot meal waiting for him on a table by his bed, he wanted to call Ann first. Then he thought of the time and realized that she would be in class, so he called his parents. His mother answered the phone, and he could hear the relief in her voice when she realized it was him.

"Oh, Shane!" she said. "Are you all right? Where are you? We were so worried. Ann is almost frantic."

"I'm in a hospital. It's a long story. For now, just know that I'm on the mend and being well looked after. The short version of the story is that I toppled into some icy water and was out in the cold for some time before I was taken into a home and looked after. I took a bad cold from the ordeal and that developed into pneumonia. Right now, I am slowly starting to get better. I put in a few bad days, but as I said, I'm on the mend now. However, I think it's going to take a little time for me to get back to full health."

"Well, Shane, I'm so glad you called. Ann will be so relieved to hear from you. She said that it wasn't like you to not call her, at least every other day. Please give her a call as soon as she gets out of class. Is there anything we can do?"

"I might have to get Dad to come up and accompany me home. I'll see how strong I am when I get out of the hospital. I'll send you the address of where I am either way."

"I'm sure he will go, for you. Just keep in touch with us, and please, call Ann as soon as possible. We love you, Shane, and please call us whenever you can too."

Elsie hung up the phone and ran to tell John the news. Once that was done, she immediately called Barbara and put her and Bill's minds at ease. It was so good to hear from him and know that he would be all right in due time.

Within fifteen minutes from the time of her call to Barbara, there was a knock at the door. Elsie turned and opened the door. It was no surprise when she saw Barbara, Bill, and Grammie standing there. She invited them in, took their coats, and ushered them into the living room.

Bill and Grammie were already settled by the fireplace when Barbara opened a bottle of wine, poured some into glasses, and carried them to the living room. They sat by the fire and talked about Shane's call and wondered what had caused him to get so sick. Since Shane told them he may need someone to escort him home, John and Bill decided they would both go, and leave as soon as they got directions from Shane. Neither one of them had ever been to Northern Quebec before, so as long as Shane was able to travel, it could be a learning experience.

That very evening, as soon as Shane felt Ann would be home from school, he called her. She was so relieved that she started to cry. She could not help herself.

"Oh, Shane, I am so glad to hear from you. I was so worried. Where are you?"

"I'm in a small hospital in Northern Quebec. I had a fall into icy water and couldn't get to a place where it was warm for quite a period of time. My clothes were wet and the temperature was below zero, so they froze to me. I developed a bad cold and within a day, it turned into pneumonia. I had a few bad days but I think I'm on the mend now. I've asked my dad to come up and accompany me home. Don't worry. I will be fine. I love you. We're getting married in less than three months, and I wouldn't miss that for anything."

"I love you too," she said with a shaking voice. "Please, get better soon and get back here where you're safe."

"Will do. I have to go now. The doctor is here. I'll tell you the whole story when I get home. I love you. Bye."

Ann hung up the phone. She was feeling much better having spoken to him and just hoped he would be fine and home soon. She went to prepare some dinner for herself and then correct some tests she had given that day. *Teaching is like housework*, she thought. *It's a never-ending job.*

Shane continued to progress and was soon sitting up for longer periods of time each day. He sent directions to his father telling him just exactly where he was, that he was starting to feel much better, and that he would soon be ready to go home. Most of his belongings were still in the cabin he had rented. He needed a change of clothes but decided he could wait until his father came to get his things and close out the cabin.

Bill Blair and John Robertson arrived within the week. Shane was up and about by this time and was feeling much better. Bill and John had closed out the deal with the cabin and brought Shane his belongings. Within minutes, Shane was dressed and ready to leave the hospital.

He was not as fully recovered as he had thought though. Even the act of getting ready to leave was tiring to him. John had rented a four-wheel drive Ford truck for travelling, and soon they were on their way.

Shane asked Bill and John if they would stop at Jean Laduc's home. He wanted to thank them for helping him and possibly saving his life. He felt that, if it were not for them, he would have frozen to death for sure.

They drove back to the Laduc's and were greeted warmly. The dog he had rescued was delighted to see him. He sat at Shane's feet and would not move. It laid its head on Shane's knee and stared up at him as though it was saying, *"Oh, please, take me with you!"*

Shane loved dogs, and even though this one had almost cost him his life, he had a special feeling for it.

"That dog really likes you," Jean Laduc said. "You know, he's not really our dog. He wandered in here one day last fall and just stayed around ever since. We'd like to find a good home for him. I think some tourist must have lost it while visiting here and left without it. The poor dog seems lost, and when we let it out, it's usually gone for some time before it comes back. I think it's looking for its owners."

Shane could not believe that someone would leave without their dog. He could never do anything like that and sat staring at it. "I am sure that dog is a purebred Nova Scotia Duck Toller," he said. "He's a beautiful animal and so good natured. I just couldn't leave him without a home. Is your daughter very attached to it?"

"Well, as you can see, we have two other dogs, and even though she likes this one as well, she's more attached to the two we had first," answered Jean.

Bill and John looked at each other. It was clear to them what was about to happen here. Shane just couldn't leave this dog. This was a neutered Nova Scotia Duck Toller, and it clung to Shane. Obviously, he would love to go home with him. It couldn't be any clearer even if it could talk. He wanted to stay with Shane.

"I'd love to have this dog. Could I take him with me?" asked Shane.

Jean looked at Shane with relief clear on his face.

"Like I said, he's not our dog. If you give him a good home, I would let you have him. He seems to like you very much. Perhaps you remind him of his former owner."

The dog stayed pressed close to Shane's leg, as if he were begging Shane to take him back home to Nova Scotia.

"What's his name?" Shane asked.

Jean shook his head. "We really don't know. We just called him 'Dog.'"

Shane ruffled the dog's fur, realising that he already knew that and his thinking still wasn't as clear as usual.

He realized that Jean was still talking. "When you take him with you, you can put a suitable name on him."

The dog looked up at him as though he was pleading to make a new home with him, and at that precise moment, the dog won. There was no way Shane could go home without him.

"Do you have a leash for him?" Shane asked.

Jean disappeared for a few minutes and returned with a new leash. The dog was already wearing a collar, with no tag, so Jean snapped the leash onto it, and then handed the leash to Shane. The dog was so excited. He jumped up on Shane, and then waited as Shane shook hands with Jean.

Shane thanked him and his wife for their hospitality and for tending to him when he needed help. Then he turned and walked out to the truck with his newly acquired friend by his side.

Bill and John stepped up and thanked the family as well, for taking care of Shane, and then said their goodbyes and followed Shane out to the truck.

It was hard to say who was happier, Shane or the dog. Shane opened the back door of the four door truck, and the dog jumped in. Shane climbed in and the dog settled beside him, putting his chin on Shane's knee and quickly falling asleep. He seemed to know he was going home at last.

They made the long trip home, and Shane was completely exhausted when he arrived. The dog nestled up beside him for the entire trip. They had stopped for two nights along the way, and except for meals, or to do his "business" outside, the dog never left his side. No one knew the dog's real name, so Shane started calling him Hector. It stuck. Soon everyone was calling him that, and it was not long before the dog seemed to realize it was his new title and answered to it.

Once Shane was home and being well cared for, he began to bounce back to his old self. Ann arrived on the weekend, and he was as happy to see her as she was to see him. Since Shane still had some strength to regain, they stayed home for the whole time she was there.

John and Elsie went home to check on things while Ann was with Shane. Hector still watched Shane's every move, but he was beginning to take a liking to Ann as well, and when Shane was not on the move, he followed Ann around. They came to the conclusion that Hector must have been owned by a couple.

It really puzzled Ann that anyone could drive off and leave their dog. She wondered if they might have been in an accident, perhaps badly hurt, and the dog ran off. He was lucky he'd come across the Laducs, who took pity on him and cared for him. He was such a beautiful, lovable dog, Ann could not help herself. She cared for Hector just as much as Shane did.

Hector had found a new family. He would be loved and looked after, and Guysborough was the perfect place for that.

Finally, Ann had to leave Shane and Hector and go back to Lawson's Brook to get ready for school the next day. John and Elsie were back and would stay with Shane to make sure that he and Hector were taken care of. John and Elsie were fond of Hector as well, and Hector was getting used to them.

He was a lucky dog, finding a home where everyone loved and cared for him. He was getting used to the property and could go out and romp around for a while, and then he was back at the door to be let in. It all worked out perfectly.

Time was passing quickly and the wedding day was drawing closer. It was now only weeks before the big day. Both bride and groom had all the things they would need for their big day, and their mothers had all the other plans looked after. All arrangements were in good hands and preparations for their wedding day were proceeding as planned.

Once Shane was back on his feet, he decided he had better take Hector to the vet for a checkup and make sure he'd had all his needles. However, before taking him there, he decided to take him to the dog spa in Antigonish for a beauty treatment. Hector got the works: warm bath, blow dry, nails clipped, and his coat trimmed and brushed until it shone. He was no longer the "shaggy dog."

He was absolutely gorgeous, and he strutted around as though he knew it was true. Next, it was off to the vet for another detailed examination. The vet checked him again for fleas or ticks, even though the lady at the dog spa had already done it. He gave Hector a complete checkup and found him to be a healthy dog. Shane told the vet how he had acquired Hector and asked if there would be any way he could check out the former owner.

"Just a minute," answered the vet. "I'll check to see if he has a microchip. That should give me some information."

The vet checked Hector and found out that he did have a microchip. He told Shane that, by scanning it, he could find Hector's home address.

Shane thought about it. Hector had a good home. Why not leave things as they were? Shane put Hector on his leash, paid the vet, and walked out, but he knew he would give it some thought. It disturbed him to know he could probably find out where the dog came from. Keeping the dog when you knew nothing about it was one thing, but keeping him when it was possible for you to know more, and return him, was something else.

Hector jumped up into Shane's truck and snuggled close to him. He loved Hector and could not even imagine giving him up. Plus, Ann and the rest of the family had become so attached to him that they would be devastated.

Shane still thought about it though. If it were his dog and he had lost him, he would want the person who found him to do the right thing. As much as he loved Hector, could he live with himself if he didn't? He decided he would wait until the weekend and talk it over with Ann.

The weekend came, and Ann arrived on Friday evening. Hector raced to welcome her the minute she walked in the door. He truly had settled in as the Robertson family dog. If he wasn't at Shane's feet as he sat writing, he was out in the yard with John or in the kitchen under Elsie's feet. As Elsie worked in the kitchen, she had to be careful not to trip over him.

Shane was still thinking about the chip and what he should do. *He is a Nova Scotia Duck Toller, and he belongs in Nova Scotia, with us.*

Later in the evening, after dinner was over and the dishes cleared away, Shane, Ann, and his parents settled in the living room. Even though it was the middle of May, it was still quite chilly, so John lit the fireplace, and it was cozy and warm.

For the first time since he'd come home from Quebec, Shane sat down at the piano and began to play. Ann picked up her violin and the two of them entertained for some time. Neither Shane nor Ann had played for a while, and they realized just how much they had missed it. Their two favourite pieces ("The Old Violin" and "Hector the Hero") closed out their evening. That was when Shane suddenly realized why he had called his newly acquired dog Hector.

The time passed quickly, and soon John and Elsie went upstairs to bed. Ann and Shane settled down for some conversation with Hector curled up at their feet, fast asleep. He never went to bed until Shane did, and then he would settle on the mat by Shane's bed. Shane told the story of taking Hector to the doggie spa and the vet. He told her that Hector had a microchip and that the vet could scan it to get Hector's former address. Then Shane put Ann on the spot, asking her what she thought he should do.

"Shane, I'm sure I feel the same way you do. I love Hector too, but I guess the proper thing to do is find out where the dog belongs. I think that, if you don't, you'll always feel guilty, and you'll never feel like Hector is really yours, even though, he was given to you. Perhaps he belongs to some little girl who keeps hoping he will come back to her."

She watched his face as he thought about her words, then, put her hand on his arm. "I'm not going to say any more. It really is your decision to make."

Shane thanked her for her opinion, and knew he would do the right thing. He just had to. If the dog belonged to some child, he could not bear the thought of keeping him or her from their beloved pet. As much as he loved Hector, he knew he couldn't live with himself if he didn't do what was right.

The very next day found Shane back at the veterinarian's to have Hector's microchip scanned. His hand trembled as he handed the leash to the vet. Shane had done some reading on the subject and knew the microchip had a number that was plugged into a database, which would give the name and contact information of the pet's owner.

Shane sat down and waited, but he didn't have to wait very long before Hector was back with him and the vet handed him the information he had asked for. Hector's rightful owner was Karl Miller, 14 Aberdeen Place, Kamloops British Columbia. There was a phone number as well.

Shane took Hector's leash from the veterinarian, paid him, and left with Hector in tow. He didn't know how he felt. He had the information he needed and knew he had done the right thing, but he couldn't bear the thought of letting Hector go. He drove home dreading the thought of calling his true owner. He decided he would do it as soon as possible. Letting it go would just prolong the agony.

Then again, he told himself, the owners may not want to take him away from a good home, or perhaps had moved, so there would be no other way to contact them. There was always the chance that Hector could stay right where he was. Shane's parents had gone back home, so the house was empty when he arrived back. He unleashed Hector when he entered the house and sat down by the phone. He sat there for a while before bracing himself and dialing the number. He heard the ring tone repeated on the line, and then a woman's voice answered.

"Hello?"

"Hello," Shane said. "Would you be Mrs. Karl Miller?"

He heard her breath catch a bit before she answered, "No, I'm not. I'm her sister. My sister, Marie, and her husband, Karl, were both killed in a car accident in Northern Quebec last summer."

"Oh no … I am *so* sorry to hear that. My name is Shane Robertson, and I live in Guysborough, Nova Scotia. The reason I'm calling is.. Well, I'm a writer and recently took a trip to Northern Quebec to collect information for a book I'm working on. When I was there, I came in contact with a family who was looking after a stray dog - a Nova Scotia Duck Toller. The dog took a real liking to me. I'm a dog lover, and I took a liking to him as well. The family who was looking after him asked me to take him, so I did. Being a dog lover, though, I couldn't help but wonder where he came from. So, I took him to our local vet, and he said that he had a microchip and he read it, giving me the name, address, and phone number of the dog's owner."

He waited for a long moment, while the woman seemed to gather herself. Finally, she said, "His name was—" She stopped, obviously still a bit shocked and confused at this news. "I mean, his name *is* Scotia. We never knew what happened to him. Is he all right?"

"Yes! Yes, he's fine. I have him here in Nova Scotia. He's settled in really well, and we all love him. How old is he?"

"Um … his papers are here in the house somewhere. Are you saying you want to keep him?"

"I would love to keep him, of course, but I just had to find out where he came from and if he was someone's beloved pet. I figured that, if he was, as much as I wouldn't want to, I'd have to give him back. He's a beautiful dog, and like I said, we all love him."

The woman sighed. "My name is Alice Lowell, and like I said, Marie was my sister. She and her husband had no children, and that dog was like a child to them. They loved him dearly, but now that they're gone… I am sure they would be glad that Scotia has a good home. I live in Australia and am just here for a short time to sell their house and close out their affairs. They had no other close relatives, or at least none who would want a dog."

"I'm so sorry for your loss. This must be a very difficult time."

"It is … but there is at least one bright light … now that I know their dog is safe, and being well taken care of and loved. Thank you! He's yours now. Please, give me your address, and I'll send you his papers."

"Thank you *so* much… I really didn't want to feel I had stolen another person's dog, but I would have been devastated if I'd had to give him up, and so would the rest of my family. I had visions of him belonging to a child though, and it would have broken my heart if I'd lost my dog when I was a youngster."

"I completely understand," she said.

"I am very sorry about your sister and her husband, but I promise I will give Hector a good home. Oh… I'm sorry, but I didn't know his name, so I called him Hector. He answers to that now. So I guess his new full name is 'Scotia Hector'. Just so you know, our local vet says that he's in perfect health. If it's okay with you, I'll write you a letter and give you the complete story of how I happened to be his new owner, and maybe some pictures of him, if you'd like."

"That would be wonderful."

When she didn't continue, Shane nodded and got down to practical matters. After waiting for her to get a pen and paper, he gave her his name again, and his address, so that she could send Hector's papers.

Then he said, "Please send me your address in Australia, and I will keep you posted on Hector's new home and owners. Thank you for taking this time and talking with me. I'll look forward to hearing from you."

"Thank you. It is so good to know that Scotia has a good home, and is well looked after. Marie would have liked that... We will keep in touch."

Shane heard a "click" as she hung up the phone.

Shane was so happy that there were tears in his eyes. As usual, Hector, who was lying on the floor at his feet while he was on the phone, jumped up, put his paws on Shane's knees, and licked his face. He seemed to know that everything was fine, and he was going to stay in Nova Scotia. The first thing Shane did was phone his parents and tell them the good news. Hector was staying! They too were delighted. They had become very attached to Hector and would have hated to see him go.

Shane phoned Ann that evening and told her the good news too. She was as happy as the rest of the family.

"We'll have a little 'Welcome to the Family' party for Hector this weekend. I'll bring Grammie down with me. You mention it to your parents, and I'll tell mine. Remember 'Hector the Hero'? That song we found in the box of Alex Blair's music? We'll play that in Hector's honour. I will pick up some wine on my way down. I can't wait until Friday. I love you. Bye!"

Friday finally arrived, and Ann picked up Grammie, stopped in Antigonish for some wine, and drove to her house in Guysborough. The Robertsons, without Shane, were already there when she arrived. Elsie told her Shane was writing and had a section he wanted to finish before he left it. He would be along shortly. To her surprise, the Fischer brothers were also there. Shane had happened to see them down at the restaurant and invited them up. They took an immediate liking to Hector. They loved dogs, but since they lived in the city and were not always at home, or even in the country, having a dog was out of the question.

Ann got Grammie settled in her favourite chair, freshened up a bit, and left for the Robertson house. It would give her a little time alone with Shane. He met her at the door as he was just about to leave for her place. He was so glad that she had decided to come up so they could talk alone. They always had so much to talk about. He told her all about his conversation with Hector's owner's sister and her guess as to how he happened to be on his own. They talked for nearly an hour, and then Shane said that they had better go or a search warrant would be sent out for them.

Barbara had a meal ready for everyone when they arrived. They ate, talked, and enjoyed their time together while Hector was stretched out on the floor at Shane's feet. When the meal was over, the ladies cleared away the dishes and loaded the dishwasher, while the men took their wine glasses and disappeared into the living room. The fireplace was lit, and it gave a nice warm glow to the room.

Ann seated herself next to Shane, and after some stories and jokes, Shane settled on the piano bench and Ann picked up her violin. They played for some time, and then Ann announced they were going to play a tune in honour of Hector's addition to the family.

They all listened intently. Not one of them, other than Grammie, had ever heard "Hector the Hero" before. When Shane and Ann finished playing it, they all clapped and remarked on how nice a piece it was. Hector wondered what all the fuss was about and jumped up and barked, as if to say, "Hey, I like it too!"

It was almost midnight when everyone left. Shane stayed back, and Ann said that she would drive him home a little later. They sat and talked about their upcoming wedding and how they were looking forward to the big day. It seemed like all the preparations were in place.

The minister from the United Church down the road was to perform the ceremony, which was to take place at the waterfalls on the Jake Sheridan property. Things were really falling into place. It had to be ready when Ann finished school on twenty-sixth of June because the wedding was on the thirtieth. She didn't have much time to correct any problems that might arise. Shane wanted to have his book completed by then and off to the printer. Things were moving along nicely.

The Big Day

TIME QUICKLY PASSED FROM May to June, and Ann and Shane's big day was quickly approaching. Ann had all the necessary tasks associated with the last days of school almost completed, and Shane had his book ready for the printers. All the necessary jobs were well on their way to being finished, and the excitement was building.

Barbara and Elsie had everything lined up for the upcoming event, and as each task was completed, it was checked off the list. They were very systematic in their approach to the responsibilities handed to them, and they left no stone unturned in carrying out their duties. They'd figured that two heads were better than one when it came to managing an event as important as this. Both of them wanted everything to be as perfect as they could make it. Even though they were not professional event planners, they felt they were somewhat qualified in their endeavours and that their natural talents would hold them in good stead.

The place for the wedding had already been settled on. Guest's cars would be left down the road a short distance from Jake Sheridan's property, and transportation was being provided to take them to the falls. Following the wedding, the guests would be taken back to their cars, and they would drive to Ann's house for champagne and refreshments.

During this time, pictures would be taken at the falls and outside on Ann's lawn, as well as some in the house. Following the pictures, there was a time for guests to congratulate the bride and groom and chat with friends, as well to listen to some of the guests who had been asked to say a few words.

Ann's matron of honour would be her cousin, Amelia, who was Bill's sister Mary's daughter. Two fellow teachers, Susan Baldwin and Sarah MacDonald, were to be her bridesmaids. Shane's best man would be Alan Foster, a good friend from his high-school days, and for his ushers, he had chosen the two Fischer brothers, Josef and Bruno. They had become good friends since their meeting at the restaurant, and Shane really liked them. They were delighted to be asked and agreed to do it without question.

The dinner was to be held at Shane's house and would be catered, making it much easier for Barbara and Elsie. They didn't have to worry about that and could enjoy the day. Shane had a very long sunporch at the back of his house, and there was plenty of room for the seventy or so guests. A band had been hired, and as soon as the tables were cleared following the dinner, there would be enough room for dancing.

Things were shaping up really well. Most of the plans for the wedding were in place. Shane's book had gone to the printers along with the book of Alex Blair's pieces of music Ann and Shane had found in the cabin. Ann would be finished at school within the week. All her clothes for the wedding and her going-away wardrobe were at her house in Guysborough. Ann was a planner. She was not one to let everything go until the last minute.

Finally, the last day of school arrived. The banquet, prom, church service, and graduation had gone off without a hitch. Ann had resigned her position there and been hired at the high school in Guysborough for the next term. This new position was the last thing on her mind as she waited for the day of her marriage to Shane.

Everything seemed to be progressing as planned, and the day could not come too soon for her.

Ann had two full days from the time school closed for the summer to the day of her wedding, and they were filled to capacity with things to do. One of the tasks she had to look after was Hector. She took him to the doggy spa where he was given the royal treatment.

He was bathed, blown dry, and had his nails clipped and filed. Then his coat was trimmed until he looked striking and then brushed until it shone. He was the most handsome Nova Scotia Duck Toller in all of Nova Scotia, and he knew it. He strutted around as if to say, "Look at me! Look at me!" The trick now was to keep him looking like that until the day of the wedding. Following his special treatment, Ann went to the pet store and bought Hector a new Nova Scotia tartan collar. If no one else was ready for the upcoming event, Hector was. He had the important duty of carrying the rings at the wedding.

Barbara and Elsie kept crossing things off the list as each part of the event was taken care of. They felt that, if everyone did their part, everything would be fine. The weather promised to be lovely, but no one could control the weather. For the past few days it had been beautiful though, so hopefully it would stay that way. If it should rain, the backup plan was to hold the wedding in Ann's house, which could work, but they were hoping it would not be necessary. They just had to keep their fingers crossed.

Finally, the big day arrived. Ann was ready and hoped Shane was as well. One of the guests was positioned at the spot where their driveways met, and when he saw Shane depart for the falls, it was his duty to inform Ann's father that it was time to leave the house. Jake Sheridan had a piper playing at the end of his driveway and one at the top of the hill as the guests headed to the falls.

As the bridesmaids came down toward the falls, Shane, his best man, and two ushers were in place, and Hector was sitting at Shane's feet, ready to perform his one duty. The bride, who was escorted by her father, was the last to take her place. Bill kissed Ann and shook hands with Shane, and then left to sit beside Barbara.

The setting was exactly as Ann wanted it. The water flowed slowly over the falls, and the sun shone brightly down on them as they said their vows. The best man had the rings held securely in his pocket, but pretended he was taking them from Hector. This was a precaution they had to take as there was the chance a rabbit or some animal could take Hector's attention and he would be gone, rings and all.

Following the ceremony, a friend of Ann's sang "Annie's Song." It was a very calm day, and the guests were certain her voice carried over the Milford Haven River. It was a perfect closure for the ceremony.

As the pictures around the falls were taken, the guests were transported to their cars, and then they drove to Ann's house where there was plenty room for parking. Jake Sheridan was the last to leave as he had to put his dogs in and lock the house before he left.

Shane and Ann arrived, and before they entered the house, there were several pictures taken out on the lawn. Hector was present for all of them. He seemed to know he was also part of the celebration and was not going to miss his chance for stardom. There were a few pictures taken in the house, and then Shane and Ann circulated among their guests.

Some time passed before one of the guests asked who played the piano. They were told that Shane did and that Ann played the violin. At the request of the guests, they played a few pieces and ended with "Hector the Hero" and Alex Blair's "The Old Violin." The guests loved it and were very much surprised by their talent. They were the perfect match in more ways than one.

They were served a delicious salmon or turkey dinner with all the trimmings and strawberry shortcake for dessert. The wedding cake had already been cut and wrapped for each guest, to eat there or take home with them. They had a terrific band, who supplied music suitable for dancing or just listening to.

Around eleven o'clock, Ann and Shane left for Ann's house to change their clothes and prepare to leave. They made a short trip back to the dance before they departed for a two-week honeymoon. For the time being, they were just going to let everyone guess where they were going. They would call their parents later. They left amid wishes for happiness and an enormous amount of confetti.

Epilogue

THIS IS NOT THE END of the story. It is just the conclusion to the book. The Blair family lived on for many years, and every year was a small adventure. Shane and Ann made their home in Shane's house. Barbara and Bill, Ann's parents, took over Ann's house, and Elsie and John, Shane's parents, built a beautiful large house on the other side of Shane's. Now there were three stunning houses, side by side by side, overlooking the beautiful Milford Haven River and all branching off the same original driveway carved out by Alex Blair. It certainly was not his intention, when he built his little cabin in the woods, that branches of his family would make their homes here.

Shane continued on with his writing and produced four bestsellers within a few years of their marriage. Ann taught mathematics at the local high school and remained there until five years after they were married, when she gave birth to healthy twins, a boy and a girl. They named them Emma Ann and Ethan Shane.

For a few years, Ann was a busy mother and loved every minute of it. Sometimes, Barbara or Elsie would help out and give her a break, but Ann didn't want to impose on them. Shane was a great help and often took time out from writing to help out.

The years passed quickly, and before they knew it, Emma and Ethan were ready for school. When this happened, Ann went back to teaching. Like their parents, both children were interested in music. Ethan wanted to play the piano like his father, and Emma took up the violin.

They were naturals and learned very quickly, and the evenings often found Ann and Shane playing along with their children. It was simple tunes at first, but it was not long before they were playing some of the tunes their parents loved. Ethan also took a liking to the guitar and soon was strumming along with Emma, and his parents. With Shane on the piano, Ethan on the guitar, and Ann and Emma on the violin, they made quite a nice little musical group. They spent many evenings entertaining their parents and grandparents, as well as some of their neighbours.

Ann and Shane, along with their two children, had a happy life together. They were delighted to be situated where they were, overlooking the Milford Haven River with their parents close by. Bill and Barbara and Elsie and John were wonderful grandparents and felt incredibly fortunate to have their children and grandchildren living near them. They spent a great deal of time together but did not interfere in the lives of their children or parents.

Grammie was getting up in years. She now lived with Bill and Barbara. However, she was never left out of any of the family gatherings. She was so grateful to have lived long enough to see her great-grandchildren and hear them play some of the tunes written by their great-great-grandfather.

Grammie often wondered if Alex Blair ever thought about what might happen to the small notes of information he'd left in the old violin case. There was a huge chance they might never have been found. If so, many pieces of this story would never have happened.

Ann and Shane were half second cousins. If it was meant to be, chances are Ann and Shane would have met and married anyway, though they would never have known their family connection before they married. How many times does this really happen in life? How many people have family connections and not know about them? Fortunately, for Ann and Shane, they were only half second cousins. Had they been first cousins, the story would have taken a much different turn.

As it was, they were a happy Blair-Robertson family living with a perfect view of a magnificent river. They lived with their two beautiful, talented children and with their parents within a stone's throw away. God was good to them. They could not ask for more.

Oh, you are wondering about Hector?

He lived a long and happy life, and it was a sad day when he passed away. As he was laid to rest on the family property, Ann and Emma played "Hector the Hero" and Etan strummed along on his guitar. One week after Hector passed away, Shane arrived home with two Nova Scotia Duck Toller puppies. Emma and Ethan named them Holly and Henry. They were two lucky dogs with a great home.

Hector the Hero is a slow air, written by James Scott Skinner (1843 – 1927). Skinner was a master Scottish fiddler and had a profound effect on Scottish music. He wrote more than six hundred compositions. He was trained in classical music, but devoted most of his life to preserving and building the folk traditions of Scotland.

About the Author

DOROTHY A. MACINTOSH IS a retired teacher and taught all grades from primary to twelve, spending most of her career teaching senior high-school mathematics. Along with teaching math, she tried to instill in her students the importance of doing your best at whatever you choose to do. Everyone has a talent—something you can do better than the average person. Find your talent; it is likely to be the one thing you really like to do. Follow a path in that direction. Do not be afraid to ask for help and do not give up. Be persistent.

Dorothy was born in Pictou, Nova Scotia, and has lived in the area all her life. She and her husband, Jack, along with their twins, Larry and Linda, showed horses for many years (Hackney Ponies) throughout Canada and the United States, ending their horse showing days with a World Champion Hackney Pony.

Life has its joys and its sorrows. In 2010, Dorothy lost her husband, and in 2015, her daughter, both to cancer. Her interests outside the family include her church, the Rebekah Lodge and being a good friend and neighbour. The main joys in her life are her son and his family, son-in-law, grandchildren, and great-grandchildren.

According to an old proverb, "Each generation will reap what the former generation has sown."

Leave the next generation something to think about, even if it's only a good laugh.

CPSIA information can be obtained
at www.ICGtesting.com
Printed in the USA
LVHW090403291120
672935LV00004B/38